THE FLAME WITHIN

"I've got to make it! I've got to make it! I've got to get word out—get word to Doc Savage!"

The man's heart pounded as he thought of the secret he carried—a secret he must reveal at once if he were to prevent untold calamity.

"The living fire! The death that cannot be avoided. The fire that spurts from within, that burns and destroys!"

Doc Savage and his **amazing crew** in a searing encounter with a phenomenon that renders even them helpless!

THE LIVING
FIRE MENACE

A DOC SAVAGE ADVENTURE
BY KENNETH ROBESON

A NATIONAL GENERAL COMPANY

THE LIVING FIRE MENACE
A Bantam Book / published by arrangement with
The Condé Nast Publications Inc.

PRINTING HISTORY
Originally published in DOC SAVAGE Magazine January 1938
Bantam edition published June 1971

Published simultaneously in the United States and Canada

Bantam Books are published by Bantam Books, Inc., a National
General company. Its trade-mark, consisting of the words "Bantam
Books" and the portrayal of a bantam, is registered in the United
States Patent Office and in other countries. Marca Registrada.
Bantam Books, Inc., 666 Fifth Avenue, New York, N.Y. 10019.

PRINTED IN THE UNITED STATES OF AMERICA

CONTENTS

THE LIVING FIRE MENACE

Chapter I

A STRANGE WARNING

The man reeled as he tried to run. His breath came in short gasps. Time after time his head twisted to dart quick, fearful looks behind him.

Perspiration was streaming from his body. His face was a queer cherry-red, the lips puffed and scarlet bright. His feet kicked up small clouds of sand.

Overhead, the sun was beating down relentlessly. On either side were cactus and sage. And ahead, not far now, were the scattered buildings of the desert town of Sandrit.

Mumbled words came from between the puffed lips.

"I've got to make it! I've got to make it! I've got to get word out—get word to Doc Savage!"

At Palm Springs, only a few short miles away, beautiful movie stars were lounging around in shorts. Cooling drinks were near at hand. The thermometer was well over a hundred.

But the running man was dressed as if for a zero winter day.

Strange wrappings on his feet accounted for part of his reeling gait. Strips from an old inner tube had been bound about those feet. The strips had cut into the flesh until blood drops marked the trail, but the man did not pause.

His body seemed sheathed in many clothes. And about those clothes other strips of rubber had been bound. On his hands were heavy rubber gloves.

But it was the man's eyes that held attention. Fear blazed from sunken orbs—deadly, unhealthy fear.

Some might have doubted that the reeling man was sane. And the words he babbled sounded like those of a man in the grip of a nightmare:

1

"The living fire! The death that cannot be avoided! The fire that spurts from within, that burns and destroys! A hell-fire! And it'll get me! I cannot escape!"

The man's heart pounded as he thought of the secret he carried—a secret he must reveal at once if he were to prevent untold calamity.

Once again his head twisted so that he looked behind him. A faint cloud of dust showed on the road over which he had just come. A big car came into view.

Frantically the man tried to run faster, his cherry-red face twisting with renewed anguish, his eyes popping.

"I've got to go on!" he gritted. "I've got to get word to Doc Savage!"

The girl in the big car did not look dangerous. She looked as if she might be one of the movie stars visiting at Palm Springs.

Long black curls framed a face that was almost perfection. Only a stub nose broke the faultless symmetry of her features. Her eyes were dark pools of bewitching enchantry. Shorts and a halter did little to hide the seductiveness of her form.

But as the girl caught sight of the reeling man ahead, her face changed subtly. An expression almost of craftiness flashed in her dark eyes; her soft lips tightened.

The man had almost reached the filling station. The girl braked the big car, slowing it instantly until it was barely moving.

The girl glanced behind her. Something like a sigh escaped her lips as she saw the road was clear.

She reached into a side pocket of the car, even as she brought the machine to a stop at the edge of the road.

Then she had opened the door, had slid to the ground, was moving rapidly toward the filling station where the reeling man had vanished. The sunlight flickered wickedly on the small, deadly automatic she carried in her hand.

The filling-station attendant did not see her. He was gazing open-mouthed at the strange apparition that had materialized before him.

The queerly dressed man seemed oblivious of the

attendant. With glazed eyes, he rushed toward the old-fashioned-type telephone in one corner of the room.

"I've got to tell them! There she is! I've got to get word to Doc Savage—"

Hands awkward in their heavy gloves, the man spun desperately on the crank to signal the telephone operator.

"Number, please," came a cool, crisp voice.

The frightened man's words tore from his swollen lips.

"Get me Doc Savage's office, in New York!" he half screamed. "Tell him this is Z-2 calling. Get Doc Savage! Get him!"

The filling-station attendant's mouth dropped open even farther. His eyes tried to jump from his head.

"Doc Savage!" he repeated, and his voice held a note of awe.

There was frenzied fear in the stranger's face, in the queer, pinched lines about his eyes as he waited for his call.

"Hurry!" he yelled impotently. "Hurry! I've got to reach Doc Savage before it's too late!"

The telephone operator was hurrying. The name Doc Savage had done something to her, also. Her voice had an unusually excited timbre as she implored intervening stations for speed.

"Doc Savage's office. William Harper Littlejohn speaking," came calm, measured tones from the other end of the wire.

The telephone operator's heart sank. "A call for Mr. Doc Savage," she said hopefully.

"Clark Savage, Jr., is absent for the nonce. I will hear the communication."

"Johnny! Johnny! Listen! This is Z-2!" the queerly dressed man shouted frantically into the telephone. "You've got to get word to Doc at once!"

He paused, subconsciously stripped one heavy glove from a hand to wipe the perspiration from his face.

"I've found something that's unbelievable! The fate of the world is at stake. And there's a plot aimed at

Doc, at all of you! Listen. I'll give you the low-down fast. I haven't got long to live. There's a living fire. It's terrible! It's—"

A pretty face pressed close to a half-opened window of the filling station. Dark eyes gleamed with sudden anticipation.

Blam!

There was a noise like two boards smacking together sharply. A queer, burned odor filled the air.

At the other end of the wire, more than two thousand miles away, that sharp crack came clearly.

But no more words came over that wire.

Chapter II

ATTACKERS STRIKE

William Harper Littlejohn, better known as "Johnny," seldom showed excitement. Lean, with a half-starved look, with glasses hiding his eyes, he appeared like just what he was: a studious scientist, one of the world's greatest geologists and archaeologists.

But he was excited now. With almost unseemly haste, for him, he signaled for the long-distance operator, barked with unaccustomed harshness:

"Get that number back, operator. Get it back at once. This is Doc Savage's office speaking!"

Across the room a thin, lean man with yellow, unhealthy-appearing skin, lounged indolently in an easy-chair. He was pulling absently at an oversize ear.

Major Thomas J. Roberts appeared a physical weakling. Appearances were deceitful, even as his slouching pose was now. He tried to seem nonchalant; actually, he was afire with curiosity.

"What is it, Johnny, some nut?" he asked.

"Nut, nothing!" Johnny rapped.

Major Thomas J. Roberts, familiarly called "Long Tom," sat up abruptly in his chair. The very fact that

Johnny had failed to use his usual quota of big words was sufficient to tell him that something was in the air.

"That was Z-2," Johnny explained rapidly. "He's an undercover agent for the Department of Justice. I once knew him well, was in the army with him. He's tripped across something big."

Swiftly Johnny repeated the message the man known as Z-2 had given him.

"I wish Doc were here," Long Tom muttered.

But Doc Savage was not near by. He was not even in the city, but was miles away, possibly thousands of miles away.

The telephone rang sharply. Johnny grabbed for it.

"I have your party back for you," the operator said sweetly.

"Z-2?" Johnny demanded breathlessly. "What happened? What was that noise—"

"Naw," came a half-frightened, choking voice. "T-this ain't that guy who called himself Z-2. H-he ain't here no more. H-he's dead. T-this is Paul Smith, the filling-station attendant."

Paul Smith's pimply face was still white. He'd witnessed something he knew he'd remember until he died—something that had horrified, yet fascinated him.

"This guy, see," he explained, as Johnny demanded details swiftly. "This guy he came in here all funny dressed. Hot as it is, he even had gloves on and had inner tire tubing wrapped around his feet for shoes."

"Go on," Johnny ordered crisply.

"His face was a funny red color, and his hand, too, when he took one glove off. I didn't think of it at the time, but I know now he was awful scared."

"I'll take that for granted. What happened?" Johnny interrupted impatiently.

"W-why, this guy, he called for Doc Savage," Paul Smith explained. "Somebody answered. He started to talk."

"Yes. Yes."

"He was awfully hot. He was wiping sweat off his face as he talked. And he really was shouting. He seemed awful worked up."

"I know." Johnny's voice became very resigned. "But tell me in words of one syllable, *what happened?*"

Paul Smith wet dry lips with the tip of his tongue.

"He—he blew up!" he shouted. "H-he just became a sheet of fire!"

There was silence for a moment.

"How did it happen?" Johnny asked softly.

"I—I don't know." Paul Smith was frankly sobbing now. "It—it was just as if a sheet of lightning hit him, or something. He—he just became one big flash of fire, like I said. He—he shriveled and burned, and the odor of his flesh, it—ah—"

"And there was nothing near him, no one close but you?"

"N-no one," Paul Smith whimpered. "It—it just happened. I—I couldn't'a' done it. No one could. I-it seemed as if the flame came from within, not from outside him anywhere. No one but I was near him, anyway."

Paul Smith thought he was told the truth. He never had seen the beautiful face of the girl that had been near the half-opened window.

Long Tom was an electrical genius. He shook his head when Johnny suggested there might have been something about the telephone that caused a short circuit or electrical discharge that could have killed Z-2.

"Impossible," he said flatly. "That could not have happened under any circumstances."

"But something did," Johnny reflected softly.

"What could a government man have been doing in a small desert town like Sandrit?" Long Tom puzzled aloud. "It had to be something big, but whoever heard of a living fire? And what was he trying to warn us about? How could we be in danger?"

Johnny shook his head. He was equally puzzled.

Long Tom and Johnny would have been even more puzzled just then if they could have heard and seen what was going on in a lavish suite at a big hotel not many blocks away.

Three men were there. One was pacing nervously up and down the room. He was a tall man, and very thin. He looked almost like a scarecrow. His face was a peculiar cherry-red. Petrod Yardoff was not well known in the United States. In some European countries he was too well known. Many strange stories had been linked with his name.

Lounging across from Yardoff was a long, husky man, with the steely, unblinking eyes of a snake. Those eyes and the gun he always carried had earned him the nickname "Stinger." Stinger Salvatore *was* well known in the United States. Many strange tales had been linked with his name, too, but none had ever been proved in court.

The third of the group watched his companions with cynical amusement. Clement Hoskins was known to very few. He intended to remain that way. Huge, with a barrel-shaped body that was as big around as he was tall, Hoskins nevertheless gave the impression of rough, vicious strength.

"You have done good work so far, Stinger," Petrod Yardoff said softly. "But one job remains. A tough job."

Stinger shrugged slightly. He pulled a handkerchief from one sleeve, wiped his hands. "Spill it," he said laconically.

"Would you like to cut in on a game that will pay off in millions?" Clement Hoskins queried sardonically.

Stinger Salvatore's lounging frame came erect suddenly. "Millions?" he repeated slowly. "The job you've got for me *must* be a tough one!"

"A tough job, but worth it—if you consider the millions," Hoskins grated. "But I wonder—I wonder if you've got nerve enough to tackle it?"

Stinger's face reddened. "Spill it!" he snapped.

"We want six men—just six," Clement Hoskins breathed.

The gangleader snorted contemptuously. "And I thought it was a tough job. How do you want 'em? Alive or—"

"Those six men," Petrod Yardoff said gently, "are Doc Savage and his five aids."

There was sudden silence in the room. Stinger's face turned the shade of paste. "Doc Savage," he muttered.

Stinger's features became sober. "Friends of mine have tried to buck that bronze devil," he said. "They've never been seen again. He's poison."

"Are you afraid?" Yardoff sneered.

The gangster looked at him with unwinking eyes. "Afraid? No," he said softly. "Just careful."

"Yet we will cut you in on a deal that's going to pay off in millions," Hoskins reminded.

Stinger took a deep breath. "Perhaps I'll try it. If I really thought you guys had anything—"

"You have a bodyguard outside, haven't you?" Yardoff interrupted.

"Why, yes. But what—" Stinger frankly showed his surprise.

"Call him in!"

Stinger hesitated for a moment. Something in Yardoff's face decided him. He called, "Rudolph!"

A typical gunman shuffled into the room. In one hand was a short-barreled .38. "Trouble, boss?" he croaked.

"No trouble, no trouble at all," Petrod Yardoff said. His lips split thinly as he walked forward, tall frame swaying. "We were merely talking about making a million dollars, and Stinger here seems a little reluctant. You wouldn't be, now would you?"

"What?" The other's pig eyes opened wide.

Stinger's jaw dropped. He started to shout. Yardoff was stripping a glove from one hand. The glove was of transparent rubber. It had been practically invisible.

The words never came from the gangleader's mouth.

Yardoff, still smiling, dropped his hand casually on Rudolph's shoulder.

There was a sudden sheet of fire. The bodyguard jerked; his mouth opened, but he made no sound. The gun dropped from seared hand. He was dead before he hit the floor.

The odor of burned flesh filled the room.

"The living fire!" gasped Stinger.

Stinger's features no longer were smooth and unruffled. They were drawn and taut. His fingers played nervously with the handkerchief in his sleeve.

Stinger had seen many men die. He wasn't afraid of

death—as long as it was some one else who was checking out.

Petrod Yardoff apparently had had nothing in his hand when he had placed it on the bodyguard's shoulder. No one else in the room had made a move.

Yet the bodyguard showed every evidence of having died from a tremendous bolt of electricity—a bolt that had covered his entire body with flame. And Petrod Yardoff, touching him, had been unharmed!

Then the gangleader saw something that had escaped his attention before. There was a thin, transparent, practically invisible rubber mask covering Yardoff's peculiar cherry-red features. His shoes were of rubber. Even the gray suit he wore was made of rubber.

Stinger had heard of the living-fire death, had heard it spoken of in awe-stricken tones in the underworld. It had been tied with whispers of a mysterious secret—a secret worth millions.

Petrod Yardoff opened a big trunk. Then he picked up the shriveled, burned form of the bodyguard, placed it in the trunk and locked the lid.

"Was the exhibition satisfactory?" he asked.

Stinger gulped. "Y-yes," he agreed reluctantly.

"We're waiting for your answer!" the barrel-shaped Clement Hoskins reminded sharply.

"Doc Savage is s-still tough medicine," Stinger protested weakly.

Petrod Yardoff turned. Once again he started to strip a rubber glove from his hand. A merciless smile split his narrow face. He started to move forward, catlike.

"No! No!" Stinger shrilled. His hand shot for a telephone. Still breathing swiftly, he made several calls in rapid succession.

"Doc Savage is out of town," he reported at last, and there was no mistaking the relief in his voice. "The two they call Johnny and Long Tom are the only ones at his office, although I understand the other three aids are around."

"Get them," the thin man said. "They'll do to start with."

"Here are your instructions," Clement Hoskins rasped. The barrel-shaped man spoke rapidly.

Stinger nodded, the color gradually returning to his face. Then he lifted the telephone receiver again, barked quick orders when he was connected with his number.

"Johnny and Long Tom first," he concluded.

Johnny and Long Tom were unaware of their danger, but they were worried.

Long Tom turned away from the compact, short-wave set in one room of Doc's suite of offices, a frown smearing his forehead.

"Can't raise him," he said shortly.

The tall geologist nodded, glanced at his watch. "I know he implicitly instructed us to make no effort to interfere with his meditations until after eight o'clock at night, but I agree with you, I wish he would reply."

Long Tom rose to his feet, shrugged. Outside it was becoming dark.

"Let's go," he said shortly. "We're due to meet Monk and Ham for dinner. Perhaps they can help us dope out what this is all about."

A high-speed elevator dropped the two aids abruptly to the basement of the big building.

In the basement they moved without words to a big, closed car. A few moments later and they were out in traffic, heading rapidly downtown.

Both of Doc's men were thinking of Z-2's queer death, of the strange warning he had imparted. Long Tom drove automatically. Johnny sat hunched in the seat, eyes half closed behind his glasses.

Even had they been alert, it is doubtful that they would have known they were being followed. Traffic was heavy, and those trailing them knew their jobs.

The shadowers were in two cars. There were five in each automobile. Each of the men had a significant bulge under the left armpit. The drivers weaved in and out of traffic with the skill of cabmen.

Doc's big car was always kept in sight.

Near Brooklyn Bridge, Long Tom swung toward the East River, angling back to strike South Street.

A little while later Long Tom swung off the smooth pavement of South Street, onto the cobblestone street that led to a sea-food tavern called Reefer's. He noticed several cars parked near by, but that meant nothing at the time. Reefer's was a popular place.

As Long Tom swung the big machine to the curb, he noticed several men alight from a car near by. One glance was all the electrical expert needed to recognize the type.

For just a moment Long Tom hesitated, his unhealthy-appearing face doubtful. Johnny was already getting out of the machine. Then Long Tom shut off the motor and opened the car door.

In that moment, the attackers struck.

Men seemed to erupt from dark doorways, from behind cars. A surging mass crashed into Long Tom and Johnny in the same instant, arms swinging, deadly blackjacks in hand.

Doc's men should have gone down under that first rush.

They didn't. Their attackers had been too anxious. They had massed too closely for their charge, got in each other's way.

A bellowed shout came from Johnny. Long Tom tried to dive back into the car. Hands grabbed him, yanked him back into the street.

Then the fight was on.

Johnny, fists swinging, head low, plunged into the men bearing down on him like a long, lean dreadnought. Speed and the very unexpectedness of his hammer-like blows, carried him across the sidewalk to a wall. He whirled, back firm against boards, clenched knuckles cracking with dazzling speed.

Long Tom sprawled forward, almost went to his knees. Still doubled up, he hit like a charging football guard. Small, weakly as he appeared, he spun men in all directions, got clear for a moment.

A swinging blackjack caught the electrical wizard across one arm, almost paralyzed it. He did not hesitate, did not pause. Lifting one big thug from his feet with a right that came from his shoetops, he made a second dive for the car.

This time Long Tom got as far as the car door before

a terrific blow caught him across the head. A shower of sparks seemed to flash before his eyes, but even as he fell he yanked a queer-shaped weapon from the car door pocket. He whirled, his finger tightening on the trigger.

There was a sound like a bullfiddle's roar. Attackers tumbled limply.

The weapon was one of Doc's own inventions. The "mercy" bullets if shot produced unconsciousness, not death; but it was as effective as a machine gun.

Long Tom was still dazed from the blow on top of his head. He could hear Johnny battling desperately. He thought only of that. He should have jumped inside the car. It had bulletproof glass, was as impregnable as a tank. From there he could have rescued Johnny easily.

Instead, he darted around the rear of the car, weapon in hand.

A small man, a wicked grin on scarred features, reared up behind him, swung a blackjack coldly and efficiently.

Long Tom went down, sprawled awkwardly on the cobblestones.

Something resembling a moan came from Johnny's tight lips. He went berserk. For a moment, his flaying fists beat back the men who crowded upon him. But he saw there was no hope. There were too many assailants.

"Help, Doc!" he bellowed instinctively.

A second later he, also, went down. A billy caught him squarely behind an ear.

Then the attackers suddenly froze.

Clear and cold came a voice. It was low, but it had a peculiar timbre, one that made it carry plain and distinctly. It was the voice of Doc Savage.

"I'll soon be there," Doc said.

Chapter III

A GIRL CALLS

But Doc Savage was far from the water-front battle scene.

His bronze skin gleaming in the reflected glow from an instrument board, his flake gold eyes intent on the story those instruments told, he was far even from civilization.

Seated in the inclosed cockpit of a speedy plane that was the type pilots call a "flying motor," Doc Savage did not appear big. But that was due to the remarkable symmetry of his body. His hair was straight, and bronze like his skin. Corded muscles showed on the backs of the hands that held the controls. His features were classic and calm. Seldom did he smile or show emotion.

The roar of the powerful motor came but faintly inside the cockpit. For that cockpit was heavily insulated. It had to be. The plane was flying thousands of feet up in the air, far up in the substratosphere. It was winging forward at nearly five hundred miles an hour.

The sound of Doc's strange, impelling voice had shocked the thugs in New York. They would have been more shocked if they had known just how far away he was when he had spoken. They would have thought it magic.

There was no magic about it. On the panel directly before the bronze man was a small television set. Above it was the speaker of a short-wave radio. A mike was near at hand.

The car Long Tom and Johnny had used was similarly equipped. Doc had seen part of the fight in New York; he had heard Johnny's cry for help. The bronze man's reply had merely come from the loudspeaker in the car his aids had occupied.

Now the bronze man was speeding toward New York. He had missed Long Tom's earlier calls. At that time he had not been in his plane.

Casual acquaintances had often wondered where Doc Savage ever found time to maintain his amazing grasp on every development of science, to study and keep ahead of a majority of those developments.

The secret was quite simple. Far in the north he had a hidden retreat—his "Fortress of Solitude." Here, when things were quiet, the bronze man would seek solitude for the tremendous concentration of which he was capable, would try new experiments, perfect new advances in medicine that would save thousands of lives, would solve some problem that had long puzzled chemists.

He was returning from such a trip now. For six months he had been apart from the world. And it was plain that he was returning just in time.

In a surprisingly short time Doc's plane dived down from the heavens to circle the lights of Manhattan. Minutes more, and it was dropping gently to the waters of the Hudson River, gliding smoothly toward the dingy warehouse that bore the sign, "Hidalgo Trading Co." Doc was the Hidalgo Trading Co. He owned the pier and warehouse.

From an adjoining pier, a small man slipped away unobtrusively. His close-set eyes gleamed wickedly in the darkness. At a corner cigar store he slipped into a phone booth, dialed a number.

"He's here, chief," he said curtly. "The bronze boy himself . . . OK . . . Yeah, I'll keep him covered."

Doc Savage had no way of knowing that his movements were being watched. Yet he moved inconspicuously as he made his way to the skyscraper where he had his offices. His private elevator shot him to the eighty-sixth floor.

In the hallway, he moved soundlessly. Just outside the door he paused, his flake-gold eyes narrowing slightly.

A faint whisper of sound came through the hallway. It was so low that the normal ear would have missed it.

Seeming almost to float, so swiftly, yet so silently did he move, the bronze man drifted down the hallway. He stopped before an apparently solid section of wall.

A low-pitched whisper came from his lips—a whisper that could not have been heard two feet away.

Instantly a section of the wall melted away and an opening appeared. Doc vanished within. The opening closed.

The bronze man was standing in one of the rear rooms of his suite of offices. It was dark, but he moved without hesitation, opened a small panel, flicked a switch.

Light glowed on a tiny screen. A desk and several chairs came into view. On the screen appeared a picture of the front office.

And in one corner, barely visible, was a crouching figure!

For several moments the bronze man studied the scene intently. Then he flicked off the small television set.

A second later, Doc opened another panel. A queer set of assorted switches came into view. Above them were two huge, oval, mercury tubes. A dull light glowed in the tubes as the bronze man pushed the switches home. A faint hum sounded for an instant, rose to a high pitch, then died out.

Doc walked over, opened the door, and entered calmly into the room where the crouching figure lurked.

A girl glanced up. In her hand she held a small, deadly automatic. Long black curls framed an almost flawless face.

She saw the opening door. She shrieked, raised her gun and fired. In the same instant she hurled two black cylinders she had in her other hand to the floor. The cylinders shattered into many pieces.

"To what am I indebted for your call?" came the low, peculiarly carrying voice of Doc Savage.

For an instant it appeared the girl was going to faint. The gun dropped from her nerveless fingers. Her dark eyes were strained wide, terror showing in their depths.

Frantically, those eyes probed every hidden recess of the room, every dark corner.

They could see nothing.

"A—a trick!" she breathed.

Strong hands caught her wrists, lifted her easily from her feet.

And if the girl had been frightened before, now she was panic-stricken. She could feel the grip of those hands, knew there must be some one there before her, some one who had grabbed her.

Her tongue stuck to the top of her mouth. She tried to scream, but emitted only a faint moan. Her eyes dropped down—and her heart seemed to stop.

She could not see her own body either. She, also, had become invisible.

She slumped, inert.

Had the girl retained consciousness, she would have understood much. She was carried to a small sofa, laid there gently. Then a *click* sounded from the adjoining room as Doc released the switches he had pressed a few moments before.

Almost immediately he became visible again.

There was nothing supernatural about any of it. The faint sound the bronze man had heard in the hallway had told him some one had broken into his office. The low whisper he had given had merely been the proper tone to operate a familiar robot, a mechanical device that opened a sliding panel in a wall that looked solid.

And while becoming invisible was not commonplace, it was something that had been done before.

The switches he had operated had released a series of short high-powered light waves, known as invisible rays. As those rays struck a human being, that human gradually vanished simply because the eye could not distinguish it when penetrated by the speeding beams. Doc had not invented the process; that had been done by Stephan Pribil, a Hungarian scientist. But the bronze man had improved it, so that invisibility came almost immediately.

The bronze man knelt beside the girl, held smelling

salts under her nose. She stirred restlessly, half opened her eyes, only to close them.

"Who sent you here?"

Doc's voice dropped even lower than usual. It held a queer, hypnotic quality.

"I—I came because I wished to."

The words came from the girl's lips dully, the voice that of a person speaking in his sleep.

"What did you wish?"

"I came to destroy a record I knew you must have. I came to keep—"

With startling suddenness the girl pulled erect on the sofa. Fear, tinged with horror, flamed in her dark eyes. One hand pressed against her lips.

"You are in no danger," Doc Savage said quietly.

The girl's eyes sought the bronze man's face.

"Doc Savage," she breathed.

The bronze man nodded. "Now if you will explain who you are, and what you desired here?" he suggested.

Fear returned to her eyes. "I—I can't! I can't!"

"But you must. It is necessary that I know. Some one has seized two of my men. I must know—"

Doc broke off suddenly. A hideous uproar had burst loose in the hallway just outside the door.

The sounds were almost indescribable. First came the lordly roar of a bull ape, a fearsome sound. It was followed instantly by the shrill grunt of an angered pig.

As the girl's lips parted and her hands clenched, there was a furious burst of fighting. The pig seemed to be going wild as it squealed in rage. The bull ape's roars increased in violence.

There was a sudden, desperate squeal from the ape, then a ripping sound, as if that ape had been torn in two.

The door burst open. A gangling figure with long, apelike arms appeared. It had a titanic chest, with practically no hips, and the small eyes were almost lost in pits of gristle. Coarse, reddish hair covered the skin.

Behind that figure came a lean, dapper man who

could have passed as a fashion plate at any time, so well was he dressed. He was waving a cane furiously, his face red with anger.

"That blasted pig can't win all the time!" he roared.

"Meet Lieutenant Colonel Andrew Blodgett Mayfair, known as Monk for quite obvious reasons," Doc said, with just a suspicion of a smile. "Pursuing him, dressed in the latest mode as usual, is Brigadier General Theodore Marley Brooks, more often called Ham."

There was sudden silence. The girl's glance went from one to the other of the newcomers with quick comprehension.

"Monk" stopped as if he had run into a ten-ton truck. A slow flush crept over his homely face.

"Ham" grinned openly, his anger disappearing as quickly as it had come. It always amused him to see Monk get flustered in the presence of a pretty girl.

"It was this ape here making all the noise," he explained maliciously. "Somewhere he found an out-of-work radio imitator who taught him to make those hideous sounds. He's been making them ever since, always pretending he's a pig licking an ape."

"At least he hasn't been able to figure out any way for the ape to lick the pig," Monk put in. His thin, childlike voice always came as a shock to those who first heard it. It sounded so out of place compared with his hulking frame.

Doc said nothing for the moment. Monk and Ham were always fighting each other when there was no one else to fight. Their quarreling dated far back to War days.

Yet despite the fact that they never seemed to work, Ham was known as Harvard's gift to the legal profession, an outstanding attorney; and Monk was a gifted chemist.

"What happened to Johnny and Long Tom?" Doc asked quietly.

Levity faded from the faces of the other two.

"That's what we really came up here to see if we could learn," Ham said seriously. "For some reason, they seem to have been kidnaped. I don't think it's anything serious, although I don't know.

"We were to meet them for dinner at Reefer's. We got there just after they'd been seized. Was quite a fight, from what witnesses told us. They were taken off toward the piers at the lower end of South Street, and probably put in a boat. We searched without finding a clue."

"Unless one remark we heard means something," Monk piped up. "I talked to a kid who was close to the car that carried Long Tom and Johnny away. He told me something that he said he'd overheard that sounded as if he was having a pipe dream."

"What was that?" Doc asked swiftly.

"He said he heard one of the crew say: 'I wouldn't want to be these guys. They're gonna see the menace of the living fire.'"

A gasp came from the girl. The three whirled toward her.

Her eyes were wide and staring. Her lips moved, but no sound came. Once again she fainted.

Chapter IV

STINGER STRIKES

Two men stood just outside the door of the office. One was Petrod Yardoff. He took a small, cup-shaped instrument away from the door, took headphones from his ears.

"We are just in time," he whispered.

His companion shuddered slightly. He was also dressed in rubber clothes, but so well were those clothes made that few would have guessed their composition. Thin, flesh-colored gloves covered his hands; tennis shoes were on his feet.

"This will be all that is asked of me?" he quavered.

"This will be all, Meeker," Yardoff said. His thin lips twisted sardonically. "After this, you will be— free."

The other's shoulders bunched; a shrewd gleam flashed for a moment in deep-set eyes.

"I am ready," he said.

"Good." One of Yardoff's hands slipped unnoticed into a pocket. It came out holding a small vial. As he talked swiftly, his fingers loosened the cork. A white liquid poured out, seeped under the feet of his companion.

"Be sure you make the argument strong enough," Yardoff concluded. "Tell just enough of the truth to arouse Doc Savage's interest. That is all that is—"

His companion waited for no more. His lips came together firmly. He opened the door, walked into the bronze man's office.

Ham spun; the end of his cane slipped off to reveal a long, deadly sword. Monk, leaning over the girl, whipped erect, jerked to his feet, long arms swinging.

"Watch the girl, Monk," Doc said quietly.

The newcomer closed the door carefully behind him. His face was working with some strange emotion.

Then fear flashed over the rubber-clad man's face; his features changed from a queer cherry-red to the color of chalk. He danced wildly from one foot to the other.

"Watch out, Doc!" he screamed. "I was sent here to try to lure you to California, to Sandrit. I was told I'd be free if I did that. I've been tricked! I'm going to die!"

Saliva trickled weirdly from the corners of his mouth.

"Don't go to Sandrit! Stay far away from there. The menace of the living fire protects it, kills all—"

The words broke off in a scream.

There was a sudden flash of fire—fire that came from inside the man's rubber suit. The man's body jerked violently; his eyes almost popped from his head. The odor of burned rubber and burned flesh filled the room.

The man fell. He was quite dead.

A peculiar, trilling sound filled the room. It seemed to come from no particular place, yet from everywhere. It was the sound Doc Savage unconsciously made when he was surprised.

With Monk and Ham at his heels, he darted to the side of the fallen man.

Outside, Petrod Yardoff smiled thinly as once more he replaced his listening device in his pocket. He had expected his companion to try to double-cross him, to try and give a warning.

That had been just what he wanted. From what he had heard of Doc Savage, the bronze man now would leave no stone unturned until he had tried to solve the mystery.

"But what caused it?" Monk's childlike voice was filled with wonderment.

"A bolt of lightning!" Ham snapped impatiently.

"The results are about the same at any rate," Doc agreed quietly. "Do you notice that the rubber suit he is wearing is untouched on the outside? The fire that destroyed him came from within."

"And he mentioned the menace of the living fire," Monk breathed. "Say. That's what that kid said Johnny and Long Tom was gonna have to face."

The bronze man nodded soberly. "I am afraid they are in great danger," he said slowly.

Monk jumped up, fairly danced about. "Then let's get going! What are we waiting for?"

"Do you recognize this guy?" Ham asked suddenly.

Doc inclined his head. "He was Darren Meeker, once a very great scientist," he said. "Meeker killed a man some years ago, and was committed to an asylum."

"And escaped about four months ago, very mysteriously. It happened while you were away," Ham added.

"Holy cow!"

The expression came in an awed tone of voice. Doc glanced up.

A huge man stood in the doorway—a man a good six feet four inches tall, who must have weighed over two hundred and fifty pounds. His face was severe, the mouth thin and grim. That mouth was set tightly now, the features puritanical. Bony monstrosities of fists hung at the end of enormous arms.

"You're just in time, Renny!" Monk howled.

"But what—"

Swiftly, Ham sketched what had occurred. The puritanical look grew even more severe on the face of Colonel John Renwick. One huge fist smacked into an equally big palm, as if he were trying to batter down a door—one of his favorite pastimes.

"You say this fellow just walked in, bellowed a warning, then went up in fire?" he asked wonderingly.

"Right!" snapped Ham.

"*Hmm.*" The corners of "Renny's" mouth drew down disapprovingly. "I wonder. Don't seem likely. But I wonder if that girl I saw going down the stairway could have had anything to do with this. She sure was a beauty, but beauty doesn't always—"

A howl came from Monk. His piglike eyes were staring with complete disillusionment at the sofa where the girl had been.

That sofa was empty now. The girl was gone.

Doc turned, looked at Monk. The hairy chemist's eyes dropped.

"Yeah, I—I know," he apologized weakly. "I was supposed to watch her. But I got excited—"

"The girl may not hold the key to this mystery, but I am sure she has information that we need," the bronze man said slowly.

"And this ape let her get away," Ham jeered.

Doc walked over to a small, square box on the desk. He opened the back, took out half a dozen slips of paper, handed one each to Monk, Ham and Renny.

"But—but these are pictures of the girl," Renny said.

"Right." Doc's voice was matter of fact. "I tried out this new camera while she was here. Complete prints are made in the matter of seconds and dropped through a slot into the rear of the camera to dry."

Renny's mouth dropped open, but he said nothing. He had seen too many of Doc's inventions to be greatly surprised.

"That girl was from the West. Her accent showed that," the bronze man went on. "She must be stopping at some hotel. Check each one, find out where she is, and find out what she knows."

As the door closed behind the three, Doc went to a bookcase near the far wall. That bookcase had been pulled out, disclosing a niche that held a machine.

The machine was a telephonic monitor, and recorded all telephone conversations. No disks were on the monitor now, however. The girl had found them. They were shattered on the floor.

The bronze man worked swiftly. Soon the disks had been put together again.

Doc played them over. He heard Z-2's conversation with Johnny. He heard Johnny's conversation with the filling-station attendant.

For a moment the bronze man's flake gold eyes were half closed. He went to the telephone, placed a call. A few minutes later and he was talking to the youth at the Sandrit filling station. He asked only one question. His queer, trilling sound filled the room at the answer he received.

Soon afterward Doc left the building.

Doc Savage had friends in many places. Thus it was that he had no difficulty in gaining access to the morgue of the city's largest newspaper.

A newspaper morgue contains clippings from scores of papers on everything that is printed.

The editor looked at the bronze man queerly when he heard the type of clippings Doc wanted to see, but he asked no questions. Soon several folders were laid on the editor's desk.

Doc Savage ran through them swiftly. He was interested only in those dated during the last six months.

The small mountain of clippings gradually faded. At last only five remained of the many he had read.

These five the bronze man reread carefully. The stories they told came from widely separated points. One said:

San Quentin, Cal.—Ten prisoners escaped mysteriously from San Quentin penitentiary today. The men, all trustees, were tending flowers in the outer yard. In some manner they overcame and killed Herbert Yokes, thirty-two, the guard. His body, badly burned, was found shortly after the men must have escaped.

A strange feature of the case is the fact that the iron gate at the entrance to the yard seemed to have been melted as if an acetylene torch had been used, although prison officials say this was impossible.

Among those who escaped was Frederick Scone, a former university professor in chemistry, serving a life term for the murder of his wife. The others were—

Another clipping read:

Albuquerque, N.M.—A man, later identified as "Slug" Bremer, an escaped convict, was killed instantly here today when struck by a train. Bremer evidently had fallen from a freight train, on the main tracks only a mile from town, and was run over by the *California Limited*. His body was badly mangled. Strange burns that seemed to cover the entire body could not be explained by Coroner Smith.

Of the three other items, two told of more escapes, one from a prison, in which more than twenty trusties had gotten away at the same time. The second told of a break at a Missouri asylum. The third reported the mysterious death of another of those who had gained freedom.

The editor was studying Doc's face curiously. "If there is anything more I can do," he began hopefully, "or if I can get you any more information—"

"This is satisfactory, thank you," Doc said.

The editor watched him leave with a long face.

In a telephone booth in the lobby, Doc called his office. The telephonic monitor had been put back in working order. At Doc's voice, another mechanical robot put the record into operation. It repeated the last call received.

"Renny calling in to report," came the recorded voice. "I have located the girl. She is staying at the Midtown Hotel, has just come in and gone to Room 1412. I'll keep watch."

Doc hung up, started for his car in front of the building.

There was a small, private alleyway only a hundred yards from the front of the newspaper building. In this alleyway, two men were crouching.

One rubbed his hands nervously on a handkerchief, flicked that handkerchief back into one sleeve.

He spoke out of one corner of his mouth. "You're sure everything is fixed? There must be no slip-ups. I was told to get this bronze devil alive, but that's too dangerous. I want him dead."

His companion squirmed uneasily. He wore greasy overalls, and his face was smeared with dirt. He held an odd-shaped object in his hands.

"It'd take more than a miracle to save that mug," he growled sourly, "even if he is—"

He broke off as Stinger's hand came down on his arm.

Doc Savage had emerged from the building.

The bronze man glanced up and down the street rapidly.

The car at the curb was a big, inclosed job, similar to the one Long Tom and Johnny had used. The door was locked. Doc took out a key, reached toward the lock.

At the alleyway, Stinger drew a long sigh of relief. "I still wish we had the real thing to work on this guy," he muttered, "but the plaything you've got rigged up should work."

Doc inserted the key in the car door, started to open it.

Beside Stinger, his overalls-clad companion worked on the odd-shaped object he held in his hands. There was a faint, humming noise.

Doc's big figure seemed to jerk erect. Fire danced about the car. Flames crackled and jumped. Women screamed. The editor stood frozen, face vacant.

For a moment the bronze man appeared absolutely rigid. A peculiar odor filled the air.

Stinger's companion worked again on the odd-shaped object he held.

The bronze man's fingers fell nervelessly from the car door. His big frame crumpled to the sidewalk.

Stinger laughed, lips drawn back from his teeth.

"Let's go, punk!" he grated. "Things are goin' to be even hotter than that around here as soon as they learn that bronze devil is really dead."

Chapter V

A CALL TO THE MORGUE

Renny had expected Doc to receive his message. He waited for a time in the lobby of the Midtown Hotel. Waiting became tiresome.

Towering high above others in the lobby, he approached the desk. "Who's in 1412?" he rumbled.

The clerk glanced up haughtily, inspected his fingernails with elaborate unconcern. "And your business?" he asked snippily.

Renny placed one huge, bony monstrosity of a fist on the desk. He closed that fist until it looked like a rough chunk of iron.

"Did you ever hear of Doc Savage?" he asked softly. "Or"—his fist rose and fell expressively—"does this look like a better argument?"

The clerk gulped. "D-Doc Savage. Why didn't you say so? Glad to do anything for a friend of Mr. Savage. It—ah—Miss Virginia Hoskins, of Sandrit, California, is in 1412. A very beautiful girl."

Renny's mouth drew down disapprovingly. "Any one with her?"

"Yes. Ah—a Mr. Clement Hoskins, also of Sandrit, is registered in an adjoining room with a Mr. Petrod Yardoff."

"Know anything about them?"

"Ah—why yes. Mr. H-Hoskins, I understand, owns a factory of some kind in Sandrit. He is a stout, very jolly sort of fellow. Mr. Yardoff, I believe, is connected with him in a business way. He—ah—does not seem so jolly. A very slender, tall sort of chap."

Renny nodded.

Across the lobby, concealed by a pillar, a very tall, slender man jerked his head to two companions. His eyes were narrow slits. Swiftly, the three made their way to an elevator. They disappeared just as Renny turned away from the desk.

The big engineer rode the elevator to the fifteenth floor, walked down one flight, and approached 1412 with silent tread. An ear to the door, he listened carefully, but heard nothing.

He knocked softly. A faint stir sounded inside the room, then ceased. There was a buzz, which might have been a whispered conversation.

Once more Renny knocked.

A lock turned. The door opened an inch. The dark eyes of Virginia Hoskins, fright showing in their depths, appeared fleetingly.

"What did you run away for?" Renny demanded primly. "Doc wanted to talk to you."

"I—I never saw you before," Virginia stammered. She tried to push the door closed. Renny put one big foot in the opening. It was as if a small-sized gunboat had moved in.

"P-please, please go," the girl whispered.

Renny snorted. "Monk might fall for that, but not me," he announced—and pushed the door wide as he stepped inside.

A blackjack caught him expertly, squarely at the base of the brain, with force enough to crush an ordinary skull.

Renny kept on going forward—right on his face. All six foot four of the big engineer sprawled, immense arms outstretched.

Strong hands grabbed him under the armpits, yanked him inside. The door closed softly.

Ham also thought Monk might fall prey again to those dark pools of enchantry if he should encounter the girl.

The dapper lawyer was glad when he reached the Midtown Hotel that he did not see the hairy form of his friend around. Monk was good in a fight, none better; but when it came to the fair sex he quite often seemed to park his brains at home.

Ham's face showed no sign of concentration as he

walked across the lobby, but he was thinking swiftly. He also had received the robot message from Renny, and he knew the big engineer should be waiting; but Renny wasn't in sight.

Ham didn't go near the desk. If anything was wrong, some one would be sure to be watching there. He drifted back through the dining room, through a side door, and raced upstairs.

The dapper lawyer was breathing a little heavily as he reached the fourteenth floor. The climb was a long one, even for a man in perfect condition.

Then his eyes narrowed, his hand tightened on the sword cane he carried.

Lights were out in the hallway. Somewhere, close at hand, he could hear faint breathing.

Ham held his breath as long as he could. Doubled over, he reached the top of the stairs in a silent leap— and jumped to one side.

Something swished by one ear. A heavy form lunged toward him. Ham spun, fast as a dancer, jerked the long blade of his sword free from the cane.

Big arms wrapped around him. The sword was knocked from his hand to fall on the thick carpet of the hallway. Ham's elbow shot back, landed with satisfying solidness just below the ribs.

His assailant said *"Whoof!"* and put one big paw over Ham's face, almost cutting off his wind. The man made small, animal-like noises as he spun the dapper lawyer around, slugged him hard on the side of the head.

Ham's head rang. His right fist shot up, caught the other under the chin, staggering him. The hand came away from his face.

"Stop it, you overgrown ape!" Ham yelled.

The other sighed deeply. "Dang it," came Monk's piping voice, "and I really thought I'd caught something! But it turns out to be a clothing-store shyster!"

"What's happened?" Ham asked, still struggling to get his wind.

"I was watching to see when you came blundering

along," Monk complained. "I doused the lights, so if that girl did come by I couldn't see her face. Then I could talk to her. But nobody's been in or out of that room."

"Let's go. Something's wrong!" Ham rapped swiftly.

A muffled murmur of voices came from Room 1412.

"Doesn't seem like a girl's room to me," Monk muttered.

"Unless she's entertaining," Ham agreed.

He knocked loudly on the door. There was a roar of laughter from inside the room. No one answered the summons.

Monk's piglike eyes sank deeper back in his head; a scowl crossed his homely face. His fist shook the door panel.

"Beat it!" a rough voice advised.

Monk's face assumed a hurt expression. "I don't like to do this," he said, his childlike voice annoyed. "It's really Renny's job, but he ain't here. So——"

His huge fists smashed into the door panel with all his apelike strength behind the blow. The panel split. Calmly he put one hand through the opening, turned the lock and opened the door.

With Ham at his heels, Monk pushed into the room. Then they froze.

"Did Renny make a mistake in the room number?" Ham wondered aloud.

It seemed that way. Certainly no girl was in the room now. Instead, four men were there. They were seated about a card table. Chips were before them. The room was full of cigarette smoke.

The green-shirted dealer was rising from his chair. His hand started for a gun that hung in a shoulder holster.

"What is this, a raid?" he snapped.

Monk lumbered forward, long arms swinging, half crooked. One of those arms shot out. "Greenshirt's" hand was knocked from the butt of his gun; he was spun halfway around.

"You boys been playing here long?" Monk inquired mildly.

"Not that it's any of your business," sneered one of the players, "but we've been here for the last two hours."

"Yeah?" Monk's voice was deceivingly bland. "Funny. Lots of smoke in here, sure enough. But there are no cigarette butts in the ash trays—and the scent of a woman's perfume is still strong in the air."

Greenshirt's hand was lightning fast as it went for his gun. Monk hardly seemed to move.

Then Monk held the gun in one huge paw, while with the other, he caught Greenshirt by the collar, lifted him up, then smashed him down so hard the chair buckled under him.

"I really would like to play games," the hairy chemist invited plaintively.

Ham was grinning tightly. Light glittered on the bright blade of his sword cane. The other three card players had been caught flat-footed. They sat, hands partly raised, mouths open.

"I suggest we start by playing the game called Truth," Ham proposed. "We want some information as to what has happened to some friends of ours."

"Go to hell! We don't know nothing about any friends of yours," Greenshirt sneered.

Monk looked very hurt. He put his head forward, invitingly.

Without warning, Greenshirt kicked him viciously on a shin. "Dang it!" Monk howled. He danced around, one foot in the air.

Greenshirt thought he saw his chance. He ducked his head, butted Monk hard in the belly. Another of the card players grabbed a gun.

Monk, his piglike eyes blazing, caught Greenshirt by the middle, threw him across the table into the gunman. The two went down.

Without hesitation, the hairy chemist leaped after them. In the same instant, some one upset the table. It caught Ham off guard, knocked the sword cane out of his hand.

"*Hold everything, folks!*" a voice blared loudly.

The fighting ceased. Six figures halted in varied and

assorted attitudes. It was an instant before they realized the words had come from a radio loudspeaker in
the room.

Before they could resume the struggle, the voice
went on—and six pair of ears strained to catch every
word.

*"I've got hot news, folks, a flash right off the griddle
that involves two of the trusted aids of the famous Doc
Savage."*

The voice hesitated a moment, then went on with
machine-gun rapidity.

*"You all know Doc Savage, folks, that famous ad-
venturer, who, with his five aids, is always fighting
against injustice. Two of those aids will never fight
again."*

The news announcer halted dramatically.

*"A flash has just reached me from the harbor police,
folks. There was an explosion on a speedboat, an hour
ago. How many were killed has not been definitely
ascertained, as yet. But two bodies were recovered.
Those bodies were badly burned. But they were identified from water-soaked papers in their pockets.*

*"They were: Major Thomas J. Roberts, known to his
friends as Long Tom, and William Harper Littlejohn,
called Johnny. Long Tom, as you know, was a wizard
with electricity. Johnny was a famous archaeologist and
geologist.*

*"Just what caused the explosion has not as yet been
learned. A passing tugboat—"*

The voice went on. Monk and Ham were no longer
listening.

Ham's face was white. "That was no accident!" he
grated. "They were killed!"

"And I think maybe these mugs can tell us something." Monk's voice was hardly recognizable.

The gunmen were huddled together. Three had their
guns. Those weapons were in their hands, but they
looked fearful just the same.

"We'll shoot," quavered one.

Monk spun, started to advance.

"A super-flash, folks! A super-flash!" The excite-

ment in the news announcer's voice penetrated even the red haze that seemed to float before Monk's eyes.

"Doc Savage himself has met with a mishap, a serious one. Something big must be breaking, folks. This flash just came in. As Doc Savage started to get in his car in front of the Globe office, just fifteen minutes ago, there was a terrific flash. It must have been electrical. Doc Savage went down—

"Wait a minute, folks! Here it is: Doc Savage, the famous adventurer, was instantly killed tonight when he was electrocuted in some manner as he started to enter his car! His body is being taken to the morgue—"

"The Morgue! I'm going there!" Monk moaned. He turned, raced from the room. Ham was close behind, stopping only to pick up his sword cane.

Chapter VI

A CHALLENGE ACCEPTED

Greenshirt grinned sheepishly and got to his feet.

"We could'a' got 'em in the long run, but just the same, I'm glad those babies left," he said. "Let's play cards a while. The job is over with."

Cards were dealt. Chips clinked.

"What's it all about, anyway?" asked the small man with close-set eyes.

Greenshirt glanced about nervously. "Not even Stinger knows. But it's tied up with the living-fire death we heard about."

"The living-fire death!" The small man shivered. "I don't want nothing to—"

"Quiet!"

Greenshirt was tense. Perspiration appeared on his face. His head turned, an inch at a time, toward the windows that looked out over a side street. One of those windows was raised.

"You're hearing things," jeered the dealer. He riffled the cards rapidly.

"I—I thought I heard something out there," Greenshirt said shakily. He glanced at his hole card.

"Ace high, bets a dollar," said the dealer.

"I'm staying—" started Greenshirt. He glanced at the window again.

He shrieked. A high-pitched shriek of fear that froze in the roof of his mouth.

A face had appeared at the open window. It was looking in calmly, without expression. It was a bronze face. The face of Doc Savage!

The card players whirled, sat frozen as they looked at the face in the window.

Behind them, the shattered door swung wide. Stinger Salvatore walked in, two gunmen behind him.

Stinger's face went blank. He looked as if he were seeing a ghost.

"It can't be! He's dead!" Stinger gasped.

Sound of his voice seemed to break the spell. The small man with close-set eyes cursed with violent rapidity. His gun appeared in his hand, belched flame three times in swift succession.

The face at the window did not move, did not change expression.

The small man prided himself as a marksman. It did not seem possible that he could have missed at such a close distance. He was sure his bullets had struck squarely in the center of that bronze forehead.

A whimpering sound came from the gunman's lips. Once more he fingered the trigger of his gun, sent lead screaming through the window, directly at the plainly seen target.

The bronze face wavered, but did not disappear.

Stinger tried to cry out. He found he had lost his voice. His legs wanted to run but his muscles would not obey his mind.

Then a bronze thunderbolt hit!

The thunderbolt did not come through the open window. It appeared through the door that led to an adjoining room.

That thunderbolt was Doc Savage. He dived through

the door in a flying tackle. He was headed directly for Stinger Salvatore.

The small gunman rose suddenly from his chair. He was directly in front of Doc's flying figure. The bronze man struck him, crashed into the table. The table collapsed.

The room became filled with struggling, surging figures. Some were trying to fight. Some were trying to escape. A gun spoke sharply and a gunman collapsed as the bullet intended for the bronze man found another victim.

The shots had attracted attention. The hotel was in an uproar. Outside, in the hallway, women were screaming. In the distance could be heard the approaching sirens of police cars.

Doc caught two of the thugs, smashed their heads together. A third dropped as strong fingers caught the back of his neck, bringing quick unconsciousness.

Stinger went away from there. He went swiftly. He went in as close to a panic as he had ever been. The hallways were filled with frightened, milling people. It was easy for the gangleader to dart into the crowd and disappear.

The house detective burst into the room. Behind him came an avalanche of blue-clad figures, carrying riot guns.

Doc looked at them calmly. Six prone figures were scattered about the room.

"But—but Mr. Savage. I thought you were dead! The radio said so!" gulped the house detective.

Doc ignored the question in the other's voice. In calm, brief sentences, he explained that he had been looking for Renny, had been fired on by a room filled with thugs. He said nothing about Stinger.

The police were curious. They asked some questions. But they did not ask too many. They knew Doc rated high with the commissioner.

The unconscious gunmen were carted off to jail. The police restored order in the hotel.

When Doc had the room to himself, he examined it closely. Then he walked to a closet door. The door was locked. With a small instrument, the bronze man released the lock in a matter of seconds. He opened the door.

Renny was hanging inside!

The huge engineer's feet were tied. His hands were bound behind him. A gag had been thrust in his mouth, puffing out his cheeks.

Doc reached in, freed the back of Renny's coat from the hook that was holding him in the air. He took the gag from Renny's mouth.

"Holy cow!" the engineer gasped. "I thought you were dead and I was sure I was."

Renny's legs were weak. They buckled up when he tried to stand. Doc carried him easily to a bed, made him comfortable while he freed him from his bonds.

"What happened?" Renny gulped.

"I wanted people to think I was dead for the time being," Doc explained briefly. "I had the newspaper editor instruct the ambulance driver to proceed toward the morgue."

"Yeah, I know," Renny argued. "But that radio guy said you had been electrocuted. It sounded as if you had been killed just like that fellow at your office."

"No." Doc shook his head. "There was nothing mysterious about the attack on me. A high-powered electric line had been attached to my car, and the juice was stepped up through a transformer as I touched it, but I was wearing rubber gloves. I was unhurt."

Renny wiped his head weakly, sat up. He still had but little strength.

"That girl tricked me, too," he confessed. "She acted frightened, and I pushed in. Somebody slugged me from behind. I came to in the closet and heard them talking."

Doc's face did not change. "And they said they were going to leave New York at once and go to Sandrit," he contributed.

Renny's eyes bulged, his puritanical features showed astonishment. "But how—how did you know?"

"Some one wants us to go there very much," Doc said slowly. "That is self-evident. By pretending to try and keep us away, they expect to decoy us there."

"But—but that fellow who died in the office, was that his purpose?"

Doc shook his head. "No. He sincerely meant his warning. But whoever was behind him anticipated what he would say, and wanted him to say it."

"I guess we are up against clever opponents," Renny agreed.

He then told Doc what the clerk had revealed about a Petrod Yardoff and Clement Hoskins.

"I'll tear them limb from limb!" a childlike voice promised with undeniable ferocity.

"You'll do nothing of the sort. You'll leave them alive until we can find out who is behind them," a second voice objected.

Monk and Ham burst into the room.

An incredulous look of delight crossed the homely chemist's features as he saw the bronze man and Renny. Ham grinned delightedly.

"I told this hairy monstrosity from the antediluvian age it would take more than a gang of punks to get you!" the lawyer shouted.

Monk was making small noises. He walked to the window, reached out and pulled in the bronze face that floated there.

"Ectoplasm!" he snorted. "Nothing but bronze tissue cloth in many folds, cut in the form of a mask, with small gas cylinders at the top to hold it in the air."

Doc ignored the interruption. "At the start all this might have seemed a revenge plot. It does not now. Too many efforts are being made to decoy us to Sandrit."

"Will there be action?" Monk dropped the ectoplasm mask.

"We still don't know what has happened to Long Tom and Johnny," Renny reminded quietly.

Monk sobered in an instant. "We saw the two bodies at the morgue that were taken from the harbor."

"And they were those of escaped convicts," Doc put in quietly.

Ham's eyes grew large. "They were badly burned. I am sure they weren't those of Long Tom and Johnny, although identification is almost impossible. But escaped convicts—"

The bronze man nodded. "I believe that is what an investigation will show."

"And Long Tom and Johnny?"

"I am sure they are alive—at least so far. I am just as sure that it is intended they never shall be seen alive."

"I guess we'll be moving soon," Monk said, "so I'll get Habeas and—"

"I'm afraid not," Doc warned. "This fire menace is too dangerous to bring your pets along. They'll have to remain behind."

"Are we going to Sandrit then?" Renny demanded.

Doc nodded. "At once. We will accept the challenge that has been hurled at us."

Chapter VII

A WILD DRIVER

Long Tom and Johnny were alive. That was the only thing they were absolutely sure about.

They did not know where they were. They did not know who their captors were. They did not know what had happened to them. They were fairly certain, however, that they were a long way from New York.

Long Tom twisted awkwardly until he could see Johnny's bound body. The archaeologist's eyes were open behind his glasses, but they held a dazed look. Long Tom seemed even more yellow and unhealthy-appearing than before.

There was only a faint hum of noise around them. They were lying in small, smelly bunks. The walls of the room were of steel.

"We got licked," Long Tom admitted.

"I dimly recall regaining consciousness only to be anaesthetized," Johnny said weakly.

"Chloroformed," the thin electrician agreed.

"But at some time we were transported by airplane."

"I remember coming to several times in the air, but each time I got another shot of chloroform," Long Tom conceded.

"But what transpired then? All that must have been hours, possibly aeons ago."

"I think I know where we are."

"On a submarine," Johnny nodded glumly.

Long Tom turned on his side, tried to hook the ropes that bound him over the edge of the bunk.

There was no sound of Diesels. That meant the sub was running on batteries, probably submerged. The sticky heat and heavy feeling of the air bore that out.

A small door opened. Several men filed in. They were dressed in greasy dungarees. There was a military bearing about them despite their attire.

The leader had a small beard that bobbed when he talked. His lips split in a grin. He spoke with a faint accent.

"You will not try to escape, please. It is useless."

"Yeah?" Long Tom asked belligerently.

"Yes." The small beard made a short dip. "We will now assist you remove the ropes you seem to dislike."

Johnny's mouth dropped, his eyes became wide behind his glasses. Two of the seamen stepped forward, stripped off the ropes.

The small beard came up firmly.

"You will come with me, please."

The leader turned, led the way. Johnny looked at Long Tom, shrugged. He followed. The seamen brought up the rear.

Their guide led them to the control compartment. He bowed deeply, and his short beard seemed just the least bit unsteady.

"Here they are, sir," he reported.

A tall, very thin man, with piercing eyes, dressed entirely in rubber, turned slowly.

"Welcome, gentlemen," Petrod Yardoff said with a sardonic twist to his sharp lips.

Long Tom's eyes traveled over the other shrewdly. He thought of Z-2 and the way the filling-station attendant had said the F.B.I. man had been dressed.

Yardoff divined his thoughts. "Yes," the thin man murmured with mock politeness, "your unfortunate friend wore a makeshift costume for much the same reason I wear this."

A long crease appeared in Long Tom's forehead. Yardoff was perspiring freely under the nearly airtight costume he wore. His face was a peculiar cherry-red color.

"Strange," Long Tom muttered.

Johnny hunched forward, a strange look in his eyes. Others had left the control room. They were alone with Yardoff.

The thin man did not appear to be watching him. Johnny glanced at the controls. They were of a familiar type. His fist knotted behind him. He set himself for a haymaker swing.

"Don't!" Long Tom rapped swiftly.

Yardoff turned slowly, an enigmatic smile spreading his sharp lips. "I thought you might guess part of the truth, Long Tom," he complimented.

Johnny's eyes made saucers behind his glasses. He looked angrily at his comrade. "If you had only retained silence, I would have whiffed our repellent host to a land of unutterable oblivion."

Yardoff mocked him with his eyes. "Your friend saved your life," he said without interest.

Johnny looked a question at Long Tom. The electrical genius pulled the lobe of one oversize ear reflectively. "It—it don't seem possible, Johnny," he said. "But I'm afraid this guy is right."

"Naturally you are asking yourself questions," Yardoff bowed. "I have no particular reason for not satisfying some of your curiosity. Look here."

Long Tom stepped forward gingerly. He glued his eye to the twin of the periscope through which Yardoff had been looking. His breath came in sharply.

Powerful lights were illuminating the course the submarine was following. That course was a weird one.

They were in a winding, stone passageway. The top of the submarine was barely awash. The submarine was moving slowly, twisting and turning on an erratic course.

As Long Tom watched, the channel widened. For a few moments they were in a huge, underground stream. The water appeared dark and malevolent.

Stalactites hung from the ceiling of the cavern. There was an oppressive air about the scene; the searchlight appeared unable to penetrate dark crevices.

With an effort, Long Tom brought his mind back to normal. Petrod Yardoff was surveying them with a jeering, sardonic look. The electrical genius was glad when the cavern passed behind, when the submarine moved on into another dark, winding passageway.

Johnny stepped forward, took his place at the periscope. The geologist forgot all about danger. He exclaimed with sudden interest.

"This proves my theorem!" he shouted loudly. "Scrutinize those stratifications, those near the roof. Why, they are the oldest known type, and that directly beneath—why, it proves that—"

Petrod Yardoff chuckled. There was something evil, something dangerous about that chuckle.

"You will see more than that, my friend, where we are going. You will see things you will wish never existed. You are going to a strange land, my friends."

Long Tom looked unconcerned. "Doc will show up sooner or later," he scoffed. "We have nothing to fear."

A thin cackle broke from Petrod Yardoff's sharp lips. "The bronze man! He cannot even take care of himself. Even now he is walking into a trap. He and the rest of his men."

The submarine moved on, slowly, through the dark, treacherous passageway.

If Doc, Monk, Ham and Renny were running into a trap they gave no sign that they realized that fact. They were soaring westward in Doc's speedy transport plane. No words were exchanged during the trip. All were filled with a premonition of unusual danger.

In a short time the landing field at Palm Springs appeared below. Several cars were parked there, and as the crowd caught a glimpse of the bronze man descending from his ship as it rolled to a stop, they made a concerted rush toward Doc.

Doc's aids were pushed to the outskirts of the crowd in the melee that followed.

Monk's face had become a mile long. There were many beautiful girls surrounding Doc. "It's tough what Doc has to put up with," he growled.

"Yeah," chuckled Ham. "Just about what the fox said when he couldn't get the grapes."

Doc made a path through the crowd and rejoined Monk, Ham and Renny. They looked over the cars at the landing field. Several had "to hire" signs on the windshields.

Renny moved forward deliberately, glanced at each of the cars in turn. At an open car he paused.

The driver was short and chubby, with an amiable face and carefree smile. "Car, buddy?" he invited.

The four got into the car. "Where to?" asked the driver.

"Do you know a Clement or a Virginia Hoskins, at Sandrit?" Renny asked.

The driver nodded. "Sure. I know everybody in this neck of the woods. That Virginia sure is a good-looker."

He threw the car in gear, the motor roared. At the first corner, the car was doing better than forty.

Ham threw a quizzical look at Doc.

"I think this was the car we were expected to take," the bronze man said. His voice, with its peculiar carrying quality, reached the ears of his aids, but the driver did not hear.

Renny was startled. "Holy cow! How could it be?" he asked. "Nothing could happen to us in this machine."

Doc said nothing.

The fat driver, his face still cloaked in a friendly, reassuring grin, really put on the speed as they reached the open road. His passengers bounced around in the rear seat.

"I hope this mug leads us into a gang," Monk rumbled. "I'd like a fight."

Monk's childlike voice carried better than he knew. The driver heard. His ears wiggled, but he did not turn around.

They came to a road that left the main highway. The long touring car skidded as it made the bend.

Instinctively, those in the rear seat reached for something to hold onto.

The car hit sand. It skidded wildly. An observer might even have believed the driver was making it skid on purpose.

"Ouch!" Monk squealed.

He yanked his hand from the rod he had been holding, looking curiously at a finger. There was a tiny puncture near the first joint. A drop of blood appeared.

The car bucked, skidded, all but overturned. It was impossible to stay in the rear seat without holding on.

Renny tried to cry out, but his voice was lost in the wind. Ham's shoulders jerked.

Doc could have braced himself with his powerful legs, but the others crashed into him. He also was holding to a rod.

Something was happening to Monk. His head dropped. His mouth went slack. He slumped.

"Poison," Ham muttered weakly. "Poison on tiny barbs on those rods we grabbed."

Renny's huge frame sagged over on Doc. The bronze man's flake gold eyes were flickering.

The fat, amiable driver glanced over a shoulder with a grin. He straightened the car out, slowed its pace to a more reasonable speed.

Behind him, his four passengers were sprawled in awkward, unconscious attitudes.

Chapter VIII

A GUNMAN SPEAKS

"So that's the famous Doc Savage, the guy everybody is afraid of," the driver sneered. He drove on a short distance, then turned off on a road that was barely a trail.

He followed the trail until it dropped into a small arroyo. He shut off the motor, lighted a cigarette.

The hum of a second engine sounded, faintly at first, then more loudly. A big car appeared. The fat driver did not seem surprised. He motioned toward his unconscious passengers and drew a deep puff on his cigarette.

"Easy as falling off a log," he grinned.

Eight men poured out of the second car. Even though Doc and his aides were unconscious, the men approached warily. Three were carrying Tommy guns. The others had automatics.

The bronze man's eyes flickered. The fingers of one of his powerful hands were pressed tight against the arteries in his other wrist. The pressure was as effective as a tourniquet. His lips, hidden as he bent over, sucked the powerful, quick-acting anaesthetic from his veins. That anaesthetic had been injected by the point of one of the many small pin-points hidden on the hand-holds.

Doc's frame was inert, apparently lifeless.

The gunmen opened both rear doors of the touring car. Doc and his men were yanked to the ground. They fell limply.

Doc was thrown into the rear of the second car. As the attackers were lifting Monk and Ham, Doc's hand rose, loosened the top of the gas tank. A moment more and the top was replaced.

Monk was pulled up first. He was tied firmly; then, still unconscious, he was tossed into the back of the second car. Renny was bound next. More men came toward Ham and Doc, ropes in their hands.

Two of the gunmen reached over, pulled the bronze man half up. One started to loop a rope about his wrists.

That was the last that gunman knew for a long time.

Doc galvanized into action. The palm of one hand caught the gunman in the back of the neck. The man never knew what hit him. The second thug opened his mouth to yell. He was lifted from his feet, hurled bodily into the gunmen tying Ham.

The others went for their guns. An automatic spoke. A Tommy gun went into action.

The gunners had to be careful not to hit their own men. Their first shots went wide.

The arroyo where the cars were was not particularly deep, but the walls rose sheer for nearly a dozen feet. It seemed impossible for any one to escape that way.

The gunmen were not even expecting Doc to try it. The bronze man caught them unprepared.

With one leap, he was on top of the touring car. A second surge of his mighty muscles and his fingers reached the top of the canyon wall.

Hot lead tore only inches behind him as he flashed over the rim of that wall, sprawled on the ground at the top.

The Tommy guns kept up a deadly barrage. One gunman issued swift orders. A look, almost of awe, was in his eyes.

The driver of the second car, with Renny, Ham and Monk tied tightly in the rear seat, roared away.

The others made a thorough search for Doc Savage. They did not find him.

A mile away, a girl watched the scene through powerful binoculars.

She saw the gunmen hunt through sage and cactus, explore small ravines. Finally she saw them return to the touring car, drive away.

Still she watched. Her breath came in sharply as she saw a faint movement almost at the edge of the arroyo. Then Doc appeared, coming from a tiny depression. He had drawn sage over him until he was completely hidden.

The girl's hand reached for the rifle at her side. Her dark eyes held a strange expression, her lips were half parted.

She was clad in a riding habit. The trim-fitting pants emphasized her soft curves. A pulse beat rapidly in her throat, just over the collar of her flannel shirt.

For a moment Virginia Hoskins hesitated. She glanced behind her, where a groom was standing near two grazing horses. Then she pushed the rifle aside and raised the binoculars again.

She saw Doc Savage seat himself on a rock, reach

inside his shirt and bring out the belt he always wore about his body. He worked swiftly. In a few minutes he no longer looked like Doc Savage.

A faint glow of admiration came to the girl's face. The bronze man placed a cap on his head, he reversed his coat. Glasses covered his flake gold eyes.

Rising, he made for the main highway at a lope that was deceiving as to its speed. Apparently tirelessly he moved on, reached the point where the cars had turned.

There the bronze man slowed, but only for an instant. Unerringly, he turned in the direction taken by the gunmen's cars.

The girl hesitated no longer. She grabbed her rifle, ran toward the waiting groom and horses. She spoke to the groom briefly. They leaped into the saddles, cut off across the desert. The girl used her spurs hard, sending her roan recklessly onward.

Doc Savage did not see the girl. His eyes were on the road.

The glasses he wore were tinted. Through them he could see all that could be seen with normal eyes, and something more as well.

He could see a faint, irregular design, almost as if the road was marked for him.

In a way it was. When his hand had been at the gasoline tank, Doc had dropped a small powder into the fuel. This powder dissolved in the gasoline, but would not burn. It was thrown out by the exhaust.

The normal eye could see nothing, but through the glasses a clear trail was left.

The trail finally turned off onto a hard, well-packed gravel road. Sandrit had been circled. Unknown danger lay ahead.

In the space of a comparatively few hours, all five of Doc's men had been abducted. Those behind the dread events had shown cunning and cleverness. But if Doc Savage was concerned, he did not show it.

Doc might have been able to rescue his men in the arroyo. That he did not attempt to do so, was merely in line with the policy he always followed.

The attackers had been heavily armed. In a general

fight, Monk, Ham or Renny might have been killed. Doc always was willing to face death himself, but when it could be avoided he never risked the lives of his men.

His aids undoubtedly were safe, at least for the present. Had the object been to kill them, there would have been no reason for delaying the execution.

The trail left by the car's exhaust thinned, then expanded to the size of a large smudge. It was as if the car had halted there briefly.

Doc did not pause. He moved past at a steady walk, eyes still downcast.

Behind him, two men rose suddenly from clumps of sagebrush that had hidden them at the sides of the road. Submachine guns were cradled under their arms.

Slowly they raised their guns, trained them on Doc's moving figure. The muzzles were held low, aimed at the legs, as if the purpose were to disable, but not kill.

"Sherlock, hell!" one of them sneered. "Let's see that wise mug deduce this!" His finger squeezed the trigger.

Br-r-r-r-r-r-r-r!

Lead rained down the road. It hit nothing.

Even as the gunmen fired, Doc Savage vanished. He vanished with a sidewise leap that carried him clear of the road, into the surrounding brush.

The gunners rushed forward.

A small, brittle, egg-shaped object caught the first squarely on the chin. His arms went up. The Tommy gun fell to the ground. Then the gunman followed it, curling up, as if asleep.

His companion paused, startled. Strong fingers suddenly caught the gunner around the neck; thumbs pressed down hard on the back of his skull.

The machine gunner became limp.

The bronze man's expression was sober. The killers had expected him. Only tiny extensions on the glasses he wore had saved him. Those extensions protruded on either side of his face; they were mirrors. Even facing straight ahead, he could see behind him.

When Doc moved on, five minutes later, the glasses has disappeared. His features seemed covered by a two days' growth of beard. His face was putty-like, with weak lines about his mouth. He carried a Tommy gun under his arm and walked as if very weary.

Tire marks were plain in the road now. They led over a small hill. On the other side of that hill, looming starkly in the open desert, was a big building. A sign at the gate read:

HOSKINS GLASS FACTORY

The tire marks of the gunmen's car turned in there.

Clement Hoskins was peering from one of the big windows of the factory building. A cold grin was on his round face. His big, barrel-shaped figure was tense.

An angry expression flashed over his features as he saw a stooped, wavering figure approach down the road.

"The fool! What is he coming back for?" he muttered.

Hard-eyed killers were grouped about him. One shifted nervously. "Looks like Sam is suffering from a sunstroke, boss," he suggested uneasily.

The wavering figure on the road appeared to find it more and more difficult to walk. The submachine gun was trailing, held by limp fingers.

Once the man lifted his head, weakly, then dropped it again. The factory building was almost before him. High wire fences surrounded the sprawling building. Every other strand of the fence was barbed wire. "Stay out" and "No Trespassing" signs were posted at the top.

A grim, ominous silence pervaded the scene.

The only entry to the factory was through a large gate in front. At one side of the gate, built half inside, half outside the fence, was a watchman's shack.

The wavering figure headed toward the gate.

"Sam Belough! Come in here! Did you kill him?"

The voice came from within the shack. It was a girl's voice. There was a note of urgency in it—a note of almost hysterical fear.

The man with the machine gun turned slowly toward the door of the shack. Virginia Hoskins stood there, black curls framing features that were almost perfect.

A gun was in her hand. It was aimed directly at the man before her.

"Come in here! Quick! If you've killed Doc Savage—"

Without hesitation, the wavering man entered the shack.

Chapter IX

THE TRAP CLOSES

Only a few miles away, movie stars were enjoying late afternoon siestas or dressing for dinner. Ice clinked in tall glasses. A subdued hum of conversation, of polite, well-bred phrases mingled with cheerful laughter.

There was none of this in the watchman's shack. But fear was there! Stark, horrible, fear!

It showed in the set of Virginia Hoskin's lips. Her finger tightened on the trigger.

"I wouldn't shoot, Miss Hoskins," Doc Savage said quietly.

A gasp came from the girl. The gun dropped as her hands twisted frenziedly.

"Doc Savage?" she breathed.

"Perhaps it is time now for you to tell me your story," the bronze man said.

His flake gold eyes glanced about the shack swiftly. It was comfortably furnished. The walls were thick, apparently of metal, strong enough to withstand rifle bullets. At the rear, looking toward the factory, was a window. The glass appeared bulletproof. Through the window, faint activity could be seen inside the factory.

The girl took a long breath. "Perhaps I *had* better explain."

Doc nodded. He glanced through the rear window again, and began to work swiftly with his hands.

Virginia Hoskins swallowed hard. She sank limply

into a chair. "Clement Hoskins is my uncle. He is a crook," she started.

The bronze man said nothing.

"My money is invested in this factory. I have become rich, but my uncle has become even more wealthy. That aroused my suspicions. I investigated."

Doc remained silent.

"He is involved in something crooked, something so big I am almost afraid even to guess what it means. But it's linked with the living-fire death!"

Doc glanced at her politely. "Yes?"

"I heard my uncle and Petrod Yardoff plotting. They wanted to capture you and your men. I was afraid for my uncle, for such lawless acts could have only one end. I was afraid for you, for if he succeeded, you eventually would have to die."

"So that is why you attempted to destroy the record of Z-2's conversation? You wanted to keep me from becoming interested?"

The girl nodded, dumbly. "I—I saw Z-2 die. It—it was terrible! I had followed him, trying to learn what he had discovered, hoping to learn what my uncle really was doing. Then Z-2 died. My uncle and Yardoff had flown to New York. I flew after them. They—"

"Quiet!" The bronze man raised his hand suddenly.

There was a faint noise just outside the shack. A man, listening there, turned swiftly and raced toward the factory.

The bronze man's deception had been discovered.

Doc spun, face emotionless. "Speak swiftly," he said. "Our time is short."

His tone brought the girl's head up. She flushed.

"Other men were in the plane with uncle, and Petrod, horrible men." She shuddered.

Doc nodded. That explained the man who had died in his office, the two whose bodies had been found in the harbor.

"I—I didn't intend to trick your friend, Renny. He— he wouldn't listen to my warning. And I wanted to warn you, earlier today. I couldn't. One of uncle's men was with me. Now if you go on, you are doomed. All your men are doomed."

"Why?" Doc's single word snapped like a pistol crack.

The girl paled. Fear returned to her dark eyes, her lips trembled.

"They—they've been taken in there, taken down to that horrible place—" She broke off, fought visibly for control.

Her eyes turned to the window at the rear of the shack. A scream burst from her lips.

A score of men were pouring from the factory, heavily armed men. In the lead was the big, barrel-shaped figure of Clement Hoskins.

"Surround that shack! Take no chances, but get Doc Savage!" Hoskins bellowed.

The big man glanced about anxiously. The sun was dropping. Already it was dusk. Soon the swift night of the desert would arrive. But Hoskins was confident. His men had circled the shack. Nothing, no one, could get out of there unseen.

"Virginia," Hoskins rapped, "come out of there before you get killed!"

For long seconds there was no answer to that command. Then the door to the shack opened. Virginia Hoskins came out. Her face was tear-stained.

Her uncle grinned without mirth.

"Now, Doc Savage," he bellowed, "you are surrounded! You cannot escape. Surrender, and your life will be spared. Attempt to fight, and you will die!"

Silence was his only answer.

Clement Hoskins swore bitterly. He motioned to one of the killers standing at his side.

The man stepped toward the gate. A small switch was just inside. He pulled that switch down.

A brilliant, blinding light enveloped the watchman's shack. The flame sizzled, white-hot, dazzling as a lightning flash.

A second time the switch was drawn back, shot home. A second time hell-fire danced about the shack.

Clement Hoskins closed his eyes, temporarily blinded by the flash. Then he opened them.

"Go get his body, boys," he said wearily. "I'm sorry we had to do that. I could have used that guy alive, but now—"

Cautiously, the gunmen crept to the shack. Guns were ready in their hands. Flashlights were turned on. The door was thrown open. A shrill yell of surprise broke from the first man to enter.

The shack was empty!

Clement Hoskins's jaw dropped. A look of utter bewilderment spread over his flabby countenance.

"He—he couldn't'a' got away!" he bellowed.

"But he did. And I'm glad." Virginia Hoskins brushed tears from her eyes, smiled wanly.

Hoskins motioned to a gunman. "Take her!" he rapped. "Lock her up. She's getting too dangerous."

Virginia paled. She fought. She screamed. It was useless. She was carried away.

Hoskins, breathing hard, rushed into the shack. The gunman had been correct. No one was there.

"The floor is metal. The walls are lined with metal," the barrel-shaped man muttered incredulously. "Even the chairs are of metal, and connected with the floor. Enough juice went through here to fry a dozen men, but that devil escaped—"

"Could he 'a' ducked out when we was all blinded by the light?" one of the men asked, nervously.

Hoskins nodded. That had to be it. There was no other answer.

The big man jerked erect with sudden decision.

"He couldn't have gone far. He'll stay around here, trying to rescue his men. Spread out. Hunt for him."

"But—but that guy's poison. It's dark. We'll—"

Hoskins spun on the speaker. One huge paw shot out. The man soared through the air, fell sprawling, his face a crimson mass.

"Treat 'em rather rough, don't you, Hoskins?" a voice drawled mockingly.

The barrel-shaped man swung around, his hand held a gun suddenly. Then he relaxed.

Facing him was a tall, well-dressed man with the

hard face of a killer. The man drew a handkerchief from one sleeve, wiped his hands casually.

"Stinger!" Hoskins exclaimed. "How did you get here?"

The other waved one arm negligently. "Easy enough. Came by plane. Walked up while you were all busy. But where did Savage go?"

The barrel-shaped man looked at Stinger with eyes that were tight slits. A dim suspicion had flared in his brain. Doc Savage was known to be an artist at disguises. He had reached the watchman's shack in the garb of Sam Belough. This man looked like Stinger, but was it Stinger? Could it be the bronze man in a new dis—

Br-r-r-r-r-r-r-r-r-r!

A Tommy gun spoke viciously. It came from the desert, across the road from the factory. Lead whistled overhead.

Clement Hoskins's face cleared; he smiled. Doc Savage was good, no question about that; but he couldn't be in two places at once. And the bronze man had carried Sam Belough's Tommy gun.

"Glad to see you, Stinger," Hoskins said.

Hoskins's gunmen, twenty strong, spread out in a thin line. They vanished across the road, weapons ready.

Hoskins's big shoulders lifted and fell in a deep sigh. "They'll get him now," he said. "Come on in the factory."

His companion was looking about him curiously.

"You've got light, lots of light, and you must have power," he said wonderingly. "But I don't see any power lines. Where do you get your juice?"

The barrel-shaped man grinned thinly. "You'll wonder about lots of things if you stick around here. And, by the way, what did you come here for?"

The other shrugged, impatiently. "You mentioned millions, didn't you?" he drawled.

A peculiar light flashed for an instant in Clement Hoskins's eyes, and was as quickly veiled. He led the way to the factory.

In the distance, the Tommy gun spoke again.

Inside the doors, Hoskins waved his hand with ill-concealed pride.

In the rear of the rambling structure, were huge electrical furnaces. Closer at hand, were shelves stacked with glassware. The tall man's eyes narrowed slightly as he noticed some of that glassware. The handkerchief flicked from his sleeve.

"Making some rather queer things, aren't you?" he asked.

Hoskins chuckled. "We can make anything out of glass. Clothes, rope, instruments, or what have you."

He led the way to a small office. "We've got all Doc's men," he said. "When we get the bronze devil himself, we'll all be—"

Hoskins stopped, frowning. Running feet sounded outside. An excited summons came from the other side of the door.

Scowling, the big man went to the door, closing it behind him. He was gone only a few seconds.

Hoskins was smiling when he returned.

"You spoke of the glassware we make," he said. "I'm going to let you in on a secret: I'm going to show you one of our experiments."

The big man pushed the other ahead of him, toward the rear of the factory. A huge furnace was in a big room. Waves of heat swirled about them. The heat was pulsing from the furnace.

"This is where we do our testing," Hoskins said. There was an excited tremor in his voice. "Right now, molten sand is in that furnace. But in a few minutes—"

Sound of a scuffle came from outside the room. The door opened. Monk, Ham and Renny were pushed inside. Their hands were bound behind them. Gags were in their mouths.

Men pulled them along roughly. Ham kicked out; Monk struggled; Renny strained at his bonds. But they were helpless.

They were hauled to the top of a platform overlooking the furnace. An inclosed slide led from that platform into the vat where molten sand bubbled.

"Doc Savage really is a clever man," Clement Hoskins said. He spoke as if to himself. "He wasn't near that Tommy gun at all. My men found it, quite by chance. A clockwork arrangement had been attached to it, so it would fire at regular intervals."

"Yes?" His companion's features did not change, he remained relaxed.

"Yes." Hoskins's voice suddenly was harsh. Armed men were pushing into the room. Their weapons were ready in their hands.

"Yes," Hoskins repeated, "so I'm going to show you this experiment. The three men up there, the three aids of Doc Savage, are going to be thrown into that furnace. I've often wondered what the result would be, how it would affect the glass, I mean, to mix human bodies with the sand. So they are going to die, unless——"

"I see your point." The other spoke with the peculiar, low, yet carrying voice of Doc Savage. His flake gold eyes looked full into Hoskins's fat face. "You want me to help you. If I refuse, then Monk, Ham and Renny die. I understand."

"And your answer?"

The flake gold eyes swept unemotionally about the ring of armed men.

"Tell me your problem," Doc Savage said. "I will see if I can solve it for you."

Chapter X

MEN OF FIRE

Clement Hoskins's eyes narrowed slightly; his mouth tightened. For a moment he hesitated, then waved his hand. Monk, Ham and Renny, still struggling, were carried from the room.

Other armed guards stood close about Doc. They were alert, with nervous fingers on triggers.

Hoskins turned to the guards, motioned to the bronze

man. "Take him to the escape room," he ordered harshly.

Doc turned obediently as muzzles of Tommy guns were thrust in his sides. Silently he permitted himself to be herded along.

He was taken down a short flight of stairs into a small room. The floor of the room was of glass. Light glowed eerily beneath it, revealing a narrow-walled passageway.

The bronze man was thrust inside roughly. Hoskins joined him. The guards stood in the doorway, weapons raised.

"You are a clever man, very clever," Hoskins said silkily. "I am afraid you are as clever with words as with deeds."

The bronze man did not move, did not speak.

"Your men have been taken to a place from which none may escape," Hoskins said grimly. "Should they attempt it, a terrible fate awaits them. None who go where they are may return and live—unless I will it. And now, whether they live or die, whether those aids of yours burn and suffer or survive unharmed, depends entirely on you."

Time seemed to stop. The guards held their breath. Hoskins's eyes were riveted on the emotionless features of the bronze man.

"Do you wish to speak in front of all your men, or would you rather tell me what you want me to do after we are alone?" Doc asked indifferently.

The tension went out of the barrel-shaped man suddenly. He wiped drops of perspiration from his forehead. With a faint smirk, he turned to the guards.

"Go outside, close the door, but guard it well," he ordered.

The gunmen obeyed.

"I'm glad you are showing sense, Savage," Hoskins said. There was no mistaking the relief in his voice. "I would rather have you with me than against me. You are a miracle man, if ever I saw one. No one but you could ever have escaped from that watchman's shack, as far as that is concerned."

Doc's face did not change. "That was simple," he said briefly. "I knew the shack was wired. Since I am wearing rubber-soled shoes and took care to stand where my body would not form a completed circuit, I was unharmed."

The fat man nodded. "Clever. But you will need more than that to solve what I want done."

He closed his lips quickly, went to the door. It was partly ajar. He slammed it.

"Now," he began, "we'll get down to business. To begin with, have you any idea what you are up against?"

"A faint idea," Doc said frankly.

"I thought you would have," Hoskins grinned. "And that gives you some idea of the peril, also. The stuff works fast. As-fast—"

"—as this," Doc finished calmly. One big fist flashed through the air. It caught the barrel-shaped man just under the jaw. Big as he was, Clement Hoskins went out as if mowed down by a cannon ball. Doc caught him under the armpits, lowered him to the floor.

In the matter of seconds, the bronze man changed to Hoskins's garb. He padded himself with clothes, made up his face until he resembled Hoskins. He stepped to the door, quickly.

"He got rough," he said harshly as he moved from the room, closed the door behind him. "Keep him there for a time. Take no chances. I'm going below."

The guards looked startled, but said nothing. They did not penetrate Doc's disguise.

The bronze man walked on swiftly. Somewhere, near at hand, there must be a way of descent to that place of horror where his men had been taken.

Three of Doc's men actually were not far away. But to Monk, Ham and Renny, it seemed that they were in a different world.

They were in an elevator cage. And that cage was made entirely of glass. Even the cables that held it were finely spun and woven glass.

The cage was dropping slowly, very slowly. A strange, peculiar hum came to their ears.

Armed guards were crowded about them. They carried weapons made of glass. That should have held the attention of their prisoners. It didn't. They were more interested in what they could see passing on either side as they dropped downward.

The rock formation changed steadily. Streaks of copper, yellow veins of gold were passed. Tunnels showed where those veins had once been worked.

The gags had been removed. Renny exclaimed in astonishment as he saw the store of mineral wealth as yet untouched.

"Holy cow! It don't seem possible! If all this is being passed up, what can be farther down?"

Monk and Ham shook their heads. They wondered, also.

A faint smell of sulphur drifted in the air. With it was another smell, a far more unusual one. It was the odor of ozone, such as sometimes is smelled in a severe electrical storm, after a bolt of lightning, or near a powerful dynamo.

Renny looked wordlessly at the others.

The glass elevator stopped. Long shafts led back on either side. A hundred yards away one shaft led into a big, roomlike cavern. There was a thunderous, stamping noise. Blast furnaces glowed. Queer instruments and utensils were near by.

"An underground glass factory!" Monk breathed unbelievingly.

The guards who had accompanied them so far, were leaving the elevator. Other men were taking their places. It was sight of these other men that brought the short hairs up on the back of the hairy chemist's neck.

With the queer newcomers at the controls, the elevator cage again began to sink.

Down, down it went, into the bowels of the earth. And for once, not even Monk had a word to say.

There were no lights visible. Rock pressed close on either side of the shaft. Yet the elevator cage glowed with a strange cherry-red glow.

It came from the bodies of the new guards.

Other strange things were taking place far down in the depths. A long, sleek, cigar-shaped monster was rising slowly in a huge, underground stream. Slowly the big submarine eased toward the tiny dock.

Men poured from the submarine, made it fast. Petrod Yardoff appeared, his thin, scarecrow figure still clad in its rubber garments.

Long Tom and Johnny were boosted out of the tower hatch. Their hands had been tied, blindfolds were about their heads.

Guided by sailors, they were brought to the tiny dock.

"One false move, and you both will die," Petrod Yardoff warned in a strangely subdued voice. "I shall not be able to help you. We do not want you to die—yet. So please be careful."

The pair were pushed ahead. They walked up a long corridor of uncertain footing and were told to stop. Then the sound of machinery came to them. A change of air pressure told them that a great door had opened.

As the door closed behind them, Yardoff spoke: "Step ahead, carefully, then pause."

Without hesitation, Long Tom and Johnny obeyed. For minutes, it seemed, they stood motionless. There was no sound. Then their blindfolds were removed.

Above them walls glowed dully. They seemed translucent, to be admitting light from behind. But a closer examination showed the light came from the walls themselves in some unexplained manner.

Johnny's mouth opened and closed. "Most extraordinary manifestation of inspired luminescence," he muttered.

"Come on!" Yardoff snapped.

They struggled upward in a cavernous passageway. The weird light from the walls grew brighter. They wound through twisting, confusing tunnels, then passed through another great door. The portal apparently was made of lead. The men who opened it handled it carefully. They used rubber gloves of great thickness. Long Tom and Johnny were thrust inside. Both gasped.

The light was blinding. The tunnel was wider here.

There were dozens of strange-appearing men in breech-cloths. Light glowed from their reddened skins.

They were men of living fire!

"Well, I'll be—" Long Tom started.

A high-pitched voice came from around the corner. "I don't give a dang if we are in a spot!" sounded the squealing tones of Monk. "You tin-horn shyster, you just mention again that you'd like to roast a pig down here, and I'll grind you to pieces on one of these rocks!"

Monk came around the corner. He was followed by Ham and Renny.

"Howling calamities!" the chemist shrilled. "How did you birds get here?"

"We were just out for a boat ride," Long Tom said dryly. "They let us off here."

"Holy cow, but I'm glad you two are alive!" Renny boomed.

"And I'll be glad when Doc gets us out of this place," Ham muttered.

"Quite an incongruous spot for a reunion," Johnny put in. "I don't like it."

The others glanced around. They were ringed by those strange cherry-red figures. There was something ominous about their silence.

Chapter XI

A MIRACLE NEEDED

There was a steady hum in the big cavern. It did not seem particularly noticeable after a time, but at first it was deafening. Doc's aids had been shouting, much as they would do in a subway. Now they, too, became silent.

The steady hum rasped on nerves. In the ring of cherry-red men about them were those whose hands and faces twitched in sympathy with that hum.

A faint look of uneasiness was on Petrod Yardoff's

face, but he tried to look unconcerned. He was pulling rubber garments from his scarecrow body, he took the gloves from his hands, the thin, transparent rubber mask from his face.

"Move on. We'll go to the laboratory," he said.

The cherry-red men opened a path for them. They made no sound, but their eyes were full of hate. A glass weapon appeared in Yardoff's hand.

Then the party rounded a turn in the corridor. The ominous silence of the men behind them was forgotten.

"Jumping catfish!" Monk squealed. "I don't believe it!"

The tunnel-like corridor fanned out into a cavern of horrible magnificence. Pointed stalagmites of strange rock formation reached weird fingers up from the floor.

Johnny's eyes were staring. The geologist was looking at rock formations such as had never been known to science before.

Everywhere there were the strange, cherry-red men in breechcloths. Light glowed from their skins. The queer figures labored at strange tasks. Glass work benches were everywhere. At one side was a glass anvil, of steel-like hardness. A piece of glowing, blue-white rock lay on the anvil. One man held it with long glass tongs. The other swung a great sledge, also made of glass.

The piece of stone was small. The sledge undoubtedly was heavy. The sledge crashed down. The man grunted. The sledge did not break, but neither did the small piece of rock.

Then Ham's breath came in swiftly. For the first time he noticed the faces of the workers. He knew some of those faces, had seen them pictured in the newspaper. And every one was a criminal!

Yardoff leaned close to the lawyer, raised his voice above that constant hum of sound.

"That noise," he said. "It makes some of them crazy. We've got to be careful how we handle them."

Then Yardoff jerked erect. A piercing shriek rose above the humming sound.

"I can't stand it! I can't stand it!" the voice screamed.

That scream might have been a signal. All work stopped. For an instant everything hung motionless. Then there was a concerted movement.

From all sides men streamed toward Petrod Yardoff and Doc's aids!

Yardoff whipped up the glass pistol. In the lead of the advancing men was the one who had screamed. His eyes were wild, protruding from his face.

The glass pistol spoke. The man curled up.

The sharp bark of the weapon brought a momentary halt in the ranks of the attackers. Yardoff's voice rang out.

"Halt, fools! You know you cannot escape!" he shouted.

The cherry-red men started to move ahead again. They moved slowly, cautiously.

Yardoff retreated, step by step. "Get behind me, head for the near wall," he gritted at Doc's men. They obeyed.

The advancing men suddenly abandoned caution. They started to run.

Yardoff turned, sprinted toward the wall. Monk, Ham, Johnny, Long Tom and Renny followed him. They did not know what it was all about, but they did know they stood no chance if they fell into the hands of the mob.

The tall, scarecrow figure of Yardoff reached a small niche. He grabbed open a small door, yanked out a coil of hose.

Liquid shot from the hose as he turned it toward the approaching mob. The liquid fell short. It landed on the hard, orelike floor of the cavern.

But it was enough. The mob halted. A long, disappointed wail burst from a hundred lips.

With hardly a pause, the cherry-red men turned, raced back toward their work benches. Strain showed on Petrod Yardoff's features.

But blank astonishment was on the faces of Doc's

aids. For the liquid spouting from the hose was common, ordinary, everyday water!

Yardoff replaced the hose. Where the water had struck the floor little eddies of steam arose. Shortly all sign of the water had disappeared.

"I—I don't understand!" gasped Renny.

"In time you will," Yardoff said. There was a thin, merciless grin on his features. "Now we will go on to the laboratory. There will be no further trouble, not for a time at any rate. These men are like children. A slight thing will set them off. Once stopped, they forget almost as quickly."

Confidentially, Petrod Yardoff started forward, the others trailing.

A man approached at a half run. He spoke to Yardoff in a low tone. The message seemed to bring joy to the scarecrow figure. He was grinning widely as he turned.

"Wait here for a moment," he ordered. "I will return soon."

He started away with the messenger.

Johnny had eyes only for the strange rock formations. Ham was studying the features of the workers. One after another, he identified wanted criminals. Many were those who had been listed as escaped convicts in recent months. Long Tom and Renny were talking together in low tones.

A childlike grin overspread Monk's features. The chemist's little eyes glittered in their pits of gristle. He saw Yardoff and the messenger enter the corridor through which they had originally come.

Monk backed into that corridor. If he could grab Yardoff, perhaps a way out could be found. He looked ahead cautiously.

Scarcely fifty feet ahead Yardoff and the messenger had paused. Yardoff was putting his rubber clothes into a glass cabinet. Monk knew Yardoff had a glass gun. It was possible the messenger did, also. But that didn't bother him. He picked up a piece of loose rock. It was the only weapon he could find.

Cautiously he slipped along. Yardoff's back was toward him. The chemist was almost upon him when the messenger shouted a warning. And in the same instant the messenger drew a gun.

Monk hurled the rock. The messenger fell on his face. With a bellow of glee, the hairy chemist leaped forward.

Yardoff whirled. He seemed to be trying to say something, to give some warning. Monk paid no heed. He dived.

Yardoff tried to dodge. He tripped, went down.

A shout went up behind Monk. He heard other feet pounding into the corridor. The voice sounded like that of Long Tom. That voice also was crying a warning.

Monk paid no heed. With a roar, he sprang again. His huge hands closed around Yardoff's neck.

A crackling like that of high-powered static electricity burst into the air. Monk was hurled through the corridor. His hands were seared and burning. He landed flat, lay still.

When Monk regained consciousness, Johnny, Renny, Long Tom and Ham were standing beside him. Close by was Yardoff, a thin grin on his thin lips.

"This is a good object lesson, my friend," he purred. "Fortunately you chose me for the victim and not the guard. Had you touched him you would now be a charred stump of flesh. The living fire is practically exhausted from my body."

Monk struggled to his feet weakly. "How'd you do it?" he demanded. "What happened?"

Yardoff's thin smile grew larger. "You might ask your friend, Long Tom. I think he has a glimmer of the truth, although he cannot bring himself to believe it."

"It—it can't be so," Long Tom muttered.

"But it is so," Yardoff said grimly. "Now come with me."

The five men walked through the corridor with sober faces. They passed the men at the work benches, went on through another corridor until they approached a second cavern.

A blue, uneven light flashed at the far end. It was a strange, unreal light.

"Holy cow!" Renny muttered skeptically. "That looks like a nightmare."

A great pulsing, like the beating of some all-encompassing mechanical heart, came from a half-concealed chamber in the distance. A huge ball of the blue light seemed to be revolving around the walls. It danced unevenly.

Yardoff laughed. "That comes from another cavern, even deeper than this," he said. "My men do not like to go in there. They fear they will never come back. I call it the Pit of Horror."

"What is it?" Johnny demanded eagerly.

Yardoff's thin face wrinkled strangely, his eyes narrowed.

"It is the problem you have been brought here to solve," he snarled. Greed was in his voice, lust for power. "It is a problem that has defeated the best scientific brains I've been able to get so far. But you men, and Doc Savage, are supposed to be even better.

"That Pit of Horror holds a force and a material that will control the world. Some details I know. Some parts I can control; some I can't. You must solve the mystery that so far has baffled all of us, must learn how we can control what we have found."

A strange, unreal look was on Yardoff's face. It was as if a mask had dropped. A fiendish, driving lust for power was there, a merciless, satanic desire.

A breechclothed guard with a particularly brutal face appeared. Between Chicago and New York he had committed at least a hundred murders.

"Take these men to the laboratory, put them to work," Yardoff said.

The guard's mouth twisted into a snarling grin as he surveyed the new arrivals.

"Before I came here I would'a' been afraid of Doc Savage," he gloated. "Not now!"

Ham apparently didn't hear him. He was looking with amazement at his companions. Their faces, also, were beginning to turn a faint cherry-red.

"Doc Savage was supposed to be a miracle man," the guard went on. "I want to see him pull one."

"He'll soon be here," Yardoff smiled. "He's a prisoner up above. He will be brought down soon."

"I want to see him pull a miracle, too," Ham whispered. "I hope he can do it."

Chapter XII

SANDS OF DEATH

Doc was doing pretty well. And Yardoff had been mistaken. The message to Yardoff that the bronze man was a prisoner had been relayed below before it had been learned that Doc, not Clement Hoskins, had left the escape room.

The bronze man, clad as Hoskins, was striding through the underground glass factory, the first stop made by the glass elevator toward the inferno beneath.

Machinery pounded and thumped around him. Blast furnaces threw a lurid red glare over the place. The bronze man hesitated now and then, let his eyes absorb every detail of the place.

The workers there paid no attention. They were accustomed to inspection trips by Hoskins.

There was one peculiar aspect to the cavern. Great motors whirred to run heavy machinery, the furnaces glowed; but nowhere was there any sign of a power line, just as there had been no such sign in the factory above. The machines seemed to draw their tremendous forces from the thin air itself.

Perhaps Doc delayed longer than he should have. Or perhaps Hoskins's jaw had been more solid than it seemed. Hoskins should have been out for more than an hour. He wasn't.

Before the bronze man was halfway through the great workshop, a shrill alarm bell sounded. Red lights flickered in a signal board up above the main doorway.

Shouts of surprise came from the workers. One seized a telephone. His face was pallid as he dropped the receiver.

"Grab that guy!" he shouted. "The one who looks like Hoskins. That ain't Hoskins. That's Doc Savage!"

Mingled howls of rage and panic resounded in the cavern. The men dropped their work, seized heavy tools as weapons. They rushed toward Doc.

One huge fellow was faster than the rest. He showed no caution as he rushed in, swinging a heavy wrench.

The bronze man dodged easily. His powerful hands shot out, seized the huge attacker. The man hurtled through the air like some long-legged medicine ball. His soaring figure bowled over leaders of the horde rushing behind him. They fell in a heap, arms and legs tangling.

A second man leaped out. He held a glass revolver. The next instant and he, too, lost consciousness. Doc's fingers had seemed barely to flick his neck. The gun was in Doc's hand.

Doc didn't shoot. The gun was loaded with deadly bullets. The bronze man had no desire to kill. He sped swiftly toward the elevator, dodging and twisting.

A group formed near the doorway. Doc turned to evade them. There was a sudden rush from behind him. The bronze man appeared hemmed in, trapped from in front and behind.

His flake gold eyes sparkled. A route was open to one side. Without hesitation he turned that way, running lightly but with the speed of a deer.

Doc started to cross what seemed a bed of sand. Too late he saw what it really was. He twisted in mid-air, spun, tried to turn back.

He was too late. The sand gave beneath his feet like powder. Fierce heat surged up below him. The sand sucked him down as if it had been quicksand.

Doc had stepped into a sand conveyer. It led directly into a huge blast furnace in an adjoining room, a blast furnace filled with molten glass.

The bronze man's pursuers gathered about. One raised a glass revolver.

"Don't shoot, fool!" the voice of Hoskins screamed. "We need that bronze devil!"

The barrel-shaped man shouldered his way through the mob.

"You're really caught this time, Savage," he gloated.

Doc relaxed, lay flat on his back, with only his legs buried in the sand. The edge of the pit was almost within reach above his head. But that was of little good. Even if he could reach that edge, he still would have to face the pack of killers that lined the pit.

The bronze man's hands appeared relaxed. One was at his side, half hidden under the sand. Suddenly that arm shot up. It made two motions in the air.

A blinding flash filled the cavern. A second blast followed instantly. Concussion knocked men to the floor. Heavy, sulphurous smoke rolled through the cavern. Men choked, gasped for breath and ran in circles. They knocked against each other, blinded.

Hoskins realized what must have happened. He had seen Doc throw two small objects. Those objects, the barrel-shaped man knew, must have been small, concentrated thermite bombs. When the bombs struck the pyrite wall, the terrific heat of the thermite burned into the sulphur, flooded the cavern with the dense, choking smoke.

But although the fat man was not deceived, he, like the others, was blinded.

Doc alone was not.

The bronze man's eyes were closed. He popped an oxygen lozenge into his mouth. Then his long arms stretched out, he jerked forward. His steel-strong fingers caught the edge of the pit. A moment more and his feet were on firm rock.

Doc could not open his eyes because of the sulphur fumes. But that did not stop him. He moved forward swiftly, his remarkable sense of direction guiding him straight to the corridor that led to the elevator.

Two guards still stood at the elevator. They had heard sounds of the chase and of the explosion, but had not moved. Hoskins had ordered them to remain where they were. They looked surprised when they saw Doc approach, but made no move. They thought Hoskins had returned.

Doc jumped into the glass elevator, pressed the starting button and hung on. The elevator had two speeds, one very slow, one very fast. The bronze man used the fast one.

The glass car pitched downward. For a time the shaft appeared to have been hewn from solid rock. Then the rock took on a different quality. A weird, glowing surface lighted the shaft with bluish luminance. Here were other evidences of attempts at mining.

Efforts had been made to carve corridors in the rock. They had been unsuccessful. The surface appeared little more than scratched. Doc halted the car for a moment, inspected one of the mining efforts.

A faint, trilling sound came from his lips. The ore was different from any he had ever seen before. That very difference might explain why Hoskins was so eager to obtain the bronze man's services.

The bronze man started the elevator again. For several seconds it dropped swiftly. Then that drop was halted. It was halted so suddenly one of the glass-woven cables snapped; the cage bounced for an instant like some huge toy on the end of a rubber band.

The elevator had not reached the bottom of the shaft. It had been stopped by some other control, some switch operated from above. The next instant it began to ascend with dizzy speed.

The car jerked to a stop and the door grated open. It was at the mine level of the foundry cavern. Hoskins, armed men with him, rushed into the cage. The cage was empty.

"He isn't here!" Hoskins roared somewhat needlessly. "He either got all the way down or got off at one of the experimental levels below."

The brutal-appearing guard whom Doc had hurled at his fellows in the cavern fight stepped in behind his leader.

"That mug won't get far, chief," he muttered. "We got him covered here. And if he did get through the lead door, why—"

"Yes, yes," Hoskins agreed. He seemed to think swiftly. "You come with me, I'll take care of you. The others can remain here."

The brutal-appearing guard quailed. Before he could object Hoskins slammed the door of the cage. The lift shot again into the depths of the earth.

It stopped with a sickening jolt. The mine shaft terminated in a small cavern. At one side was a massive door, made of some leadlike metal.

Hoskins eyed the door for a long moment and a slow grin split his fat face. "It does not appear that he has passed through this door, although he is so damned tricky he may have figured out how to do so without leaving a sign. Go back up, keep guard."

As the elevator shot upward once more, a shadow seemed to drift into a hidden corner of the cavern. That was all. But Doc was on the scene.

He had leaped into one of the mine shafts when the cage had been yanked up. As the cage returned, bearing Hoskins to the bottom, the bronze man had ridden with it. He had ridden on top.

Hoskins turned toward the great leadlike door. A smile was on his lips. He was sure Doc couldn't get away, even if he wanted to. And he was more than certain the bronze man could not run until his men were at least safe.

The barrel-shaped one reached beside the door, pressed a hidden lever. The big portal swung open suddenly. Hoskins stepped inside.

A sudden rush of feet swept him back. A thin, rat-faced man clad in a breechcloth, his skin a cherry-red, led a dozen others similarly appearing in a rush toward Hoskins.

"We know you, Doc Savage!" he cried. "We was telephoned you was comin' down dressed as Hoskins."

Hoskins opened his mouth to speak. But the words that apparently issued from his lips brought an expression of amazement over his fat face.

"What are you going to do about it?" he seemed to say.

"I didn't say that!" he screamed in the next breath.

"I said what are you going to do about it?" Hoskins' voice repeated.

Hoskins's expression was that of a man stunned, a man who couldn't believe his own ears, and seemingly not his own voice. But it was nothing to the consternation on the ratty pan of the breechclothed thug. Some one had told him once that when Doc Savage acted mysterious, he was doubly dangerous. And this was certainly mysterious. It didn't even make sense. "Ratface" gulped.

"I ain't enjoying doing this, Savage," he shouted, "but it's the living fire if I don't!"

Hoskins's face became almost purple with apoplectic rage.

"What do you mean, you rat?" he screamed. He gulped.

"Well, get it over with, start something," he seemed to continue. "I can take all you guys!"

That was too much for Rat-face. He shouted to his fellows. Long strands, ropes of rubber and woven glass, swished through the air. They encircled Hoskins, caught him around the arms and the legs. In the end the barrel-shaped man was bound thoroughly.

The jolting brought Hoskins to his senses. He recalled then that Doc was known as an expert ventriloquist, realized the bronze man must have been close by and had thrown his voice to make it appear Hoskins was speaking when the barrel-shaped man really was not.

Hoskins looked directly at the rat-faced man. His lips moved soundlessly. Rat-face started; he looked incredulous.

Hoskins shook his head savagely. Again the lips formed words without sound.

Slowly, cautiously, almost fearfully, Rat-face moved forward. He leaned over, put a hand against Hoskins's face.

There was a faint snap. That was all.

"You—you're really Hoskins," Rat-face muttered.

"Of course." Hoskins sighed deeply. "I've been down here so often, I've taken the living fire from my body so much, that it takes only a few minutes for me to be safe here. Had you touched Doc Savage then, you know what would have happened: he would have been dead."

Rat-face was apologetic. He loosened the bonds about Hoskins with trembling fingers. "But Doc Savage is smart enough—" he began.

"No man is that smart!" Hoskins snarled. He got to his feet, whipped a glass gun from his pocket. He spoke almost in a whisper:

"Savage had to be close, or he could not have made it appear I was speaking. Search the elevator cavern closely. Doc Savage must be there. Find him!"

The cherry-red men swarmed into the room where the elevator had descended.

Hoskins watched with narrow eyes. The men were finding nothing, but a strange thought had occurred to him.

"Come here!" he rasped.

The men obeyed, returned through the lead door. Hoskins closed and secured it. When he turned, his features were hard, a glass gun was ready in his hand.

"You know that those who first enter this cavern cannot touch one of you without immediate death," he said harshly. "It is only after they have remained here a while, until their bodies have become as yours, that they are safe. Now, stand in line. Join hands!"

There was one big cherry-red man in the group. He had been the last to come from the elevator cavern. He walked to one end of the fast-forming line.

Hoskins's eyes centered on that man. He couldn't be sure, but he didn't remember any of his attackers being that big. But he hadn't counted them. If this was Doc, then he would know soon.

"All right! Join hands!" Hoskins repeated impatiently.

The big man joined hands with the cherry-red figure closest him. It happened to be Rat-face.

Nothing happened.

Hoskins's face fell. He had been mistaken.

"O.K.—" he began.

"Chief! Chief! This guy's a fake!" Rat-face was screaming the words. He was trying to free his hand from the grasp of the big man who held him.

"This guy ain't one of us!" Rat-face bellowed. "He—he's wearing rubber gloves!"

Chapter XIII

THE LIVING FIRE STRIKES

The big man at the end of the line gave a tremendous surge. Mighty muscles rippled and tightened under smooth skin. The entire line of cherry-red men were snapped through the air like a group of skaters cracking the whip on slick ice. They smashed into Clement Hoskins, knocked him from his feet.

Then the big man let go. Flake gold eyes flashed as he turned and raced down the corridor.

Doc Savage was on his way to the Pit of Horror!

Clement Hoskins was running almost before he got to his feet. Doc Savage on the loose in the underground labyrinth that surrounded the Pit of Horror did not suit him at all.

Hoskins was worried. He didn't know what the bronze man would do next.

Frantically he raced in pursuit. He stood no chance. His barrel-shaped figure was not built for running.

Hoskins soon realized that. He was panting as he reached that great cave of the workshop.

Yardoff took one look at his barrel-shaped partner. The scarecrow-shaped man halted.

"You let him get away?" he said.

Hoskins nodded. His shoulders slumped. "But—but he's down here," he said.

"Tell me what happened."

Hoskins did. "I'm afraid," he concluded simply. His breathing had returned to normal.

Yardoff's thin face narrowed in concentration. "He is smart," he said at last. "That was why we wanted him. But he is up against something he can't escape—unless we help him. We have no intention of doing that. You and I can get out of this place alive. No one else can. Sooner or later, since he is down here, we will find him."

"But—but suppose he catches us, holds us as hostages?"

"A checkmate," Yardoff agreed. He grinned venomously. "Or would be—if it wasn't for Virginia."

"Virginia?" Hoskins repeated vacantly.

"Certainly." Yardoff's face became malevolent. "She tried to save him. She has fallen for him. He knows this, and while I know he never falls for women himself, he would go to any length to save her from harm."

"So?"

"I want her." Yardoff spoke calmly, but his eyes were not nice to see. "Have her brought down. Put her on the submarine. If that bronze devil tries to disrupt our plans, we'll tell him she will die. She must be put out of the way anyway, sooner or later, because she knows too much; but we won't tell him that."

Hoskins's mouth opened and closed. He became old suddenly. But he did not argue. He turned to leave. Instructions must be given.

"No one can beat you," he said.

Hoskins might not have been so sure had his eyes been equipped with television. Two scenes might have disturbed him:

One was the figure of a great, breechclothed man gliding silently through the queerly glowing recesses of the corridors and caverns of the underground labyrinth.

Doc Savage was heading directly for the Pit of Horror!

The other scene would have shaken Hoskins even more. It was taking place at Palm Springs.

Three silver-gray transport airships had landed. It was night now. A lean, hard-appearing man was the first to descend. Unconsciously he pulled a handkerchief from one sleeve and wiped the palms of his hands.

The men who poured out of the three planes did not look appealing. They were as choice a gang of murderers as ever gathered in a single spot.

They headed toward an open touring car at Stinger Salvatore's command.

The driver of the touring car was staring at Stinger with fear-stricken countenance. Like a hypnotized chicken, he could not move his gaze from the unblinking eyes of the gangleader.

"I—I'm lost," he breathed. "Stinger is going to kill me."

The driver tried to make himself small as Stinger Salvatore halted in front of the car.

"Double-crosser!" spat the gangleader.

"I—I ain't done nothin', boss," the moon-faced driver whimpered.

Stinger's eyes glittered. "You let me get tricked," he rasped softly.

"I—I don't understand."

"Get in, boys," Stinger ordered. The gangsters poured into the machine. There were so many, some had to stand on the running boards.

"Get going!" Stinger snarled.

So nervous his hands would not hold still, the fat driver put the car into motion.

"What is it, boss?" he quavered. "What is wrong; what have I done?"

"You let Hoskins and Yardoff pull a fast one on me!" Stinger cracked.

"But—but—"

"Yardoff and Hoskins came to me and talked of millions," Stinger explained softly. "They wanted me to get Doc and his men for them. I got two of them. And what happens?"

"I—I don't know."

"That was what they wanted to happen. As soon as they get the two guys, Yardoff and Hoskins go on their own. They never intended to cut me in, to begin with. They're giving me the run-around. And I had you here to keep me posted. You didn't. You let them make a sap out of me."

The fat driver wet dry lips. Stinger was right. Hoskins had paid him more than Stinger, had told him not to say anything about Doc Savage arriving. He tried, now, to clear himself.

"Doc and three of his men got here this afternoon," he muttered. "They were overpowered and captured."

"Good!" snapped Stinger. "Now I'll get the whole crowd."

If the driver hadn't given reports to Stinger before, he tried to make up for it now. The crooks on the running boards grinned. It always amused them to see some one else trying to talk his way out of being murdered.

The factory soon came into view. "Stop here!" rapped Stinger.

The crooks got out of the car. It was strange how many musicians there appeared to be. Nearly all were carrying violin cases.

"I—I can go now?" trembled the driver.

"Sure," said Stinger. As calmly as if he were butchering a chicken, the gangleader pulled out a silenced revolver and shot the driver. A round hole showed in the driver's forehead. He fell on his face.

"Okay, boys," Stinger said. "You know what to do. Let's go!"

"I wonder what we're going to find here," said one killer to his companion. "This whole set-up is a screwy one!"

The gunman would have thought things were more screwy than ever if he could have seen Doc Savage just then.

The humming drone of disembodied power roared in his ears. In addition, now, there was a queer pulsing in the air.

Doc was proceeding slowly. The manner in which the bronze man stopped, examined every inch of queer rock formation around him, indicated he was trying to find the answer to some vital problem.

The bronze man stopped, looked at his hands and arms. His skin tingled with an odd, galvanizing sensation, was turning an actual cherry-red under the cherry-red dye he had used to hide his distinctive bronze coloring.

In the long, twisting passageway behind him a face showed for an instant. It disappeared when Doc stopped. As the bronze man went on, a stealthy figure crept slowly in pursuit.

Doc's ears were keen. But the constant humming drone was sufficient to drown out any other noise. He did not know he was being followed.

The figure behind him was neither the barrel-shaped one of Hoskins, nor the scarecrow figure that was Yardoff. Indeed, this one looked furtively behind him as often as he looked ahead. Whatever was his purpose, it seemed it was entirely his own.

Doc went on. He turned a corner. His bronze skin seemed to turn a livid blue. A large cavern lay before him. The air that filled it seemed to be a burning, livid blue. It was as if the cavern were a great mercury arc lamp. In the midst of this danced a great ball of even more brilliant blueness. It rocked about unevenly like a weird will-o'-the-wisp of hell.

The bronze man stood still for a moment. Then cautiously, he crept forward. He stopped, peered over a high ridge in the floor of the cavern.

Then he saw the wall of living fire!

A great, jagged wall of rock seemed to blaze with smokeless flame. The will-o'-the-wisp ball seemed to draw its strength from there. The humming noise was almost deafening. The pulsating vibration was strong enough to make the flesh quiver.

And at the bottom of that wall of living flame was the Pit of Horror.

Doc did not need to be told. The evidence was there. A heap of skulls lay suggestively at one side. But that was not what made the scene so loathsome. It was the pile of bodies that had not yet become skeletons that appeared fearsome.

The men were dead. They had been dead for some time. Flame played over their bodies, flame that sparkled and shot out tiny streams of sparks.

Doc's strong hands grasped the top of the ledge before him. He raised himself slightly for a better look as a faint, trilling sound came from his lips, sounded even over the pulsating roar.

Then it happened.

Strong, ghostly hands seemed to grasp the bronze man. His fingers, steel strong, grabbed at the ledge of rock.

Those fingers were not strong enough. So fast that his body itself seemed a streak of light, Doc was picked up from the ledge. He was jerked through space.

With a loud, smacking impact the bronze man was literally sucked hard against that wall of living flame.

He hung there, midway up a smooth, perpendicular surface. There were no obstructions near him. His arms were outflung, but they were limp. Like a fly impaled on a pin, he was suspended. Flame flickered over his body. His eyes were glazed and unseeing.

Back in the corridor, soft footsteps drew closer. A figure dodged furtively behind a rock. A mirthless chuckle drifted through the air.

Chapter XIV

A PROFESSOR PLAYS TRICKS

Doc's five aids were in the laboratory cavern. For a long time they had nothing to do. They could only look, while guards lounged near by.

The laboratory was worth inspecting. It was different from any they had ever seen before, but only in one respect: Everything was made of glass. In addition, however, it was as well equipped as even the best scientist could ask.

But just looking grew palling. And Doc's aids were not the kind to remain worried for any length of time. Even the guards grinned as Monk and Ham bickered.

"Enter, the scarecrow," grinned Ham. The others looked up. Yardoff was approaching.

"I see you couldn't catch Doc," Monk gibed.

Yardoff's eyes grew hard, but he ignored the remark. He held out his hand to Long Tom. In his palm was a small piece of queerly glowing rock. He said:

"Your job is to discover the atomic structure of this substance. Do not waste time. Your lives and the life of Doc Savage depend upon your success."

Yardoff dropped the small piece of rock in Long

Tom's hand. Long Tom jerked in surprise. The rock was heavy—heavy beyond all proportion to its size.

His exclamation caught Monk's interest. Johnny moved forward, eyes lighting.

Yardoff grinned slightly. "I'll leave you in charge of my very able assistant, Professor Torgle," he said.

"Holy cow!" said Renny.

There was reason for his astonishment. The man who came from behind Yardoff would have attracted attention anywhere.

His feet headed one direction, his body another, as if some giant had at one time twisted him halfway around. His head was unbelievably flat on the top. Little eyes that had no color of their own, glowed like tiny red coals. The mouth looked like a ragged slit cut by a knife into a dull piece of red leather.

"I hope you boys are as smart as you're supposed to be," he said. The voice was a mirthless cackle.

Yardoff disappeared.

"In this laboratory," continued Professor Torgle, "you are all at my mercy. I have not been able to solve the secret of the power rock, so I have amused myself making death traps, that never fail. Make yourselves at home, gentlemen."

Ham was studying Professor Torgle with particular interest. Torgle had been one of the most dangerous criminals the world had ever encountered. He had been particularly dangerous because he was a scientist of more than ordinary ability, with a sharp, keen brain.

Torgle supposedly was in an asylum, but he wasn't. He was here.

Renny moved toward the queer-shaped professor.

Ham barked gutturally in a tongue that made Torgle's head snap around. It was the language of ancient Maya.

Professor Torgle's small eyes flamed with quick anger. "Plotting against me, are you?" he cackled. He gestured toward one side of the cavern.

Almost behind Ham was an enormous electric chair. It looked not unlike the one in Sing Sing's death house, save that it was larger and made of glass. There were metal contact plates in the seat, on the arms and on the high back.

"Watch!" screamed Torgle.

Whipped about by an invisible force, Ham found himself suddenly seated in that chair.

An expression of amazement came over the dapper lawyer's face. Clamps of glasslike substance snapped around his legs and arms.

"Now get to work, do what you were told to do!" Torgle screamed. "The lawyer is of no use down here anyway. So I will keep him here until you have finished."

Ham had not been plotting against Torgle when he spoke in Mayan. He had been warning them to be careful, not to arouse the queerly shaped man, that it might be dangerous.

"Let's get to work," Long Tom urged. "It looks like that is the best we could do for all concerned."

Ham did not appear to be in particular danger. And since he wasn't, the expression on the dapper lawyer's face was almost laughable.

The hairy Monk was scowling, however, as he followed the others to a work bench. He'd like to get the scrawny neck of Professor Torgle between his fists.

Monk spread an array of test tubes out before him, began to tinker with chemicals. Johnny and Long Tom pressed close by.

Renny wandered about. He was an engineer. The others were much better equipped for this job than he was.

Monk applied various chemicals to the piece of glowing rock. Nothing happened. It seemed insoluble in anything. He used a diamond drill on it. The diamond point wore flat. The rock was harder than the diamond.

Then with Johnny, he put the chunk in a small electric furnace. Long Tom turned the power on full. The indicator needle shot up. It went far beyond the melting point of any rock or metal they had ever heard of. Then they cooled it, took out the crucible holding the glowing chunk.

The piece of ore was as unscathed as if no heat had been turned on it at all!

"Howlin' calamities!" Monk shrilled. "I can't believe it!"

"A phenomenon of extraordinary possibilities," the geologist murmured. "If it could be smelted or milled, it would be an impregnable metallic substance."

"You boys ain't doin' so good," cackled Professor Torgle.

Monk growled to himself. Long Tom was bending over another bench. He had pulled about him a complicated array of indicator dials, induction coils, high-voltage batteries and transformers.

Renny was idling in the direction of the electric chair. He looked over a shoulder. Torgle's attention seemed centered on the experiments the others were making.

The big engineer dived toward Ham. If he could only get those big hands on the fastenings that held the lawyer down, he was sure he could free him.

A startled shout broke from the engineer. His severe-appearing features contorted with pain. He halted as if he had smashed into a wall in mid-air.

Torgle turned around, chuckled hideously. Monk looked up just as Renny went to the floor.

Monk bellowed like an enraged bull. He plunged toward Torgle. The queer-shaped man scuttled backward with unexpected speed. He reached a lever, pulled it.

Monk also stopped as if he had slammed flat against an invisible wall. He struck it with such force that he knocked over a large glass work bench.

The work bench did not go all the way to the floor. It stopped, tilted far over, as if held up by invisible hands.

Renny got to his feet, an incredulous expression on his disapproving face. Monk's arms were crooked, his piglike eyes flaring.

Torgle laughed.

"That is a high-frequency ray of greater voltage than man has ever known," he chortled. "Another one surrounds your friend in the electric chair. You are helpless."

Monk's face was grim. He understood how high-frequency rays worked. They set up an invisible wall, and this one had been as strong as steel.

Long Tom alone had gone on with his work. He labored with a feverish intensity. He hauled one huge step-up transformer before him, adjusted a complex array of coils and dials.

Experimentally he pulled a lever. There was a sharp, whirring sound, and crackling sparks shot from the step-up transformer. The electrical wizard shut it off, adjusted another dial. Then he pulled the lever down again. A tight smile spread over his face.

The whirring was louder this time. The crackling sparks shot many feet into the air. Then the whirring became a hum.

A sharp crash came from behind them. The crazily leaning work bench had fallen to the floor. Ham leaped from the electric chair.

The high-frequency rays which had formed the invisible wall had been broken.

Torgle howled in surprise. He hadn't thought these aids of Doc Savage could penetrate the mystery of his devices.

Renny started for him. The queer-shaped professor shuffled rapidly backward. Long Tom spoke swiftly in Mayan. Renny stopped.

"We've still got to figure out what this is," Long Tom reminded.

"Yeah and Ham is no use to us, you should'a' left him where he was," Monk grumbled.

"You didn't do so hot yourself," Ham gibed.

Monk leaped toward him. Ham danced out of the way, seized a glass knife and brandished it in front of him.

"I'll carve slices off that hairy hide of yours!" he yelled.

Professor Torgle looked on with open mouth. "Get to work!" he screamed.

A faint grin was on Long Tom's face. As Torgle's attention was centered on the struggling pair in the center of the laboratory, the electrical genius moved toward the panel of levers the professor had been operating.

"Okay, boys," he yelled suddenly, "get him! I've got his control board. He's helpless!"

Torgle yelled with rage. The mock fight in the center of the room stopped. The four aids all raced toward the professor.

"Stop! Stop!" howled Torgle.

"Stop nothing!" said Ham. "I'm going—"

Professor Torgle pressed a concealed button. The effect was amazing.

Doc's aids stopped as if they had been suddenly frozen. They seemed to hang grotesquely in the air. They looked like motion-picture films of runners suddenly halted in the projector. Long Tom's hands hung motionless over the levers on the panel board.

The five might have been living statues. They could not move; they could not speak.

A strange light flickered in Professor Torgle's sunken red eyes.

"Fools!" he cackled. "If you had used brains, if you had solved the secret of the strange stone, we all would have been free men. Now you will remain here and die. But not me."

With his queer, sidling walk, Torgle slipped from the laboratory cavern. He went toward the Pit of Horror.

At the ledge he peered over. Doc Savage's body still hung, suspended against the wall of living fire. The professor laughed horribly. It had been he who had trailed the bronze man to this place.

"The others fear, and rightly," he chortled, "but not me. And now I have the famous Doc Savage at my mercy."

Carefully, his strange method of walking making his task more difficult, Torgle descended directly into the Pit of Horror. He paid no attention to the fearsome heap of bodies.

Without hesitation he walked to the wall of living

fire. His fingers sought tiny projections. He pulled himself up, an inch at a time.

As he hung beside Doc's suspended body, he took a glass knife from his breechcloth. He lifted the knife, held it back of Doc's neck, the arm poised for a thrust.

His tiny eyes danced with wild glee.

Chapter XV

KILLERS CLASH

Clement Hoskins would have been worried if he could have seen Doc then. Not that he cared about the bronze man's health, but he needed him alive, needed Doc's brains.

But just then Hoskins wasn't even thinking of Doc. He had other worries.

Yardoff, his thin face venomous, was listening to a telephone description of things happening above ground. His eyes glittered dangerously. Armed gangsters were creeping upon the glass factory. One of the thugs on guard above thought he had recognized Stinger Salvatore.

Rapidly Yardoff told Hoskins what he had heard. Hoskins's moon face hardened savagely.

"It is time," he said, "that we eliminated Salvatore anyway. He has outlived his usefulness."

Yardoff nodded. "The fact that he is attacking without warning shows he realizes we intended to do that."

Hoskins rolled his barrel-shaped body toward one of the queerly glowing walls of the cavern in which they stood. There, above a rubber plate on the floor, protruded two short handles.

Hoskins seized the handles, kicked a lever with his feet. The ruddy complexion of his face turned a bright crimson. Sweat poured from his fat pores. He stood there, silent, for more than a minute. Then he released his grip and turned to Yardoff.

"Just a precaution," he rapped. "I have a plan."

The two strode toward the leaden door that opened onto the elevator shaft. As they passed it, Hoskins pressed a button and the whine of machinery announced the descent of the glass cage.

From a small locker, Hoskins took out rubber shoes, rubber gloves and outer clothing. Yardoff did the same. The cage jolted to a stop. The two got in.

"Perhaps," Yardoff grinned thinly, "we can talk suitable terms with this ambitious gangster."

The lift shot upward.

The thugs in the glass factory did not know how many attackers there were. One of them, a huge, broken-nosed individual, had seen a dozen or more slinking figures. Suddenly he brought a machine gun to his shoulder, pressed the trigger.

Br-r-r-r-r-r-r-r!

Stinger had one less cohort. The broken-faced killer grinned. This was going to be simple. Only an artillery attack could take the glass factory.

The killer looked out the window again. He saw a queer-looking weapon poke out from behind a pile of sand. It wasn't a machine gun. It had a heavy gauge and a queer, pineapple-like protuberance.

There was a loud *bang!* and the protuberance disappeared. It hurtled through the window, scarcely an inch from the skull of "Broken-nose."

Boom!

The glass factory rocked as the bomb exploded. Broken-nose lost all interest in proceedings. Parts of his body splashed on the walls. Two other thugs dropped, dying.

Fear gripped the survivors. Machine guns were one thing. Fighting against virtual trench mortars was something else again. The factory walls were not built to withstand an attack of that kind.

"Those guys are tough," whined one. "Maybe we'd better—"

He didn't finish his sentence. He saw Hoskins and Yardoff emerge from the elevator. Their appearance was more terrifying to him than the weapons in the hands of the attackers outside. He changed his mind about suggesting that perhaps they should join forces with Stinger Salvatore.

Hoskins conferred briefly with Yardoff and barked quick orders. Men lined the windows with deadly Tommy guns. Their death roar filled the air. Bursts of sand kicked up in front of the factory. Occasionally a scream announced a bullet had found its mark.

Powerful searchlights, sheltered by bulletproof glass, made the scene outside as light as day.

Hoskins drew in his breath sharply. The attackers had come prepared.

A dozen armed thugs were creeping across an open space. Lead beat about them. But they were unharmed. They were pushing ahead of them prow-shaped shields of metal. The shields were so constructed that they deflected machine-gun slugs without injury to the men behind them.

The boom of grenades grew louder, like the bass notes to the higher whine of the Tommy guns in the symphony of death. Lethal bombs crashed through factory windows. One entered the open mouth of a blast furnace.

The explosion spewed molten glass out into the room. Men screamed in agony, covered with burning torment. The stench of singeing flesh filled the room.

Three blasts came in rapid succession. They were not inside the factory. They were just outside. Barbed wire leaped into the air.

A path through the death-charged strands had been cut by the exploding grenades.

The defending thugs cast frantic, desperate looks at Yardoff and Hoskins. Yardoff glanced at his barrel-shaped companion, nodded.

Without a word, Hoskins pulled a great white sheet of cloth from a locker, hung it from a window.

"Cease firing!" Yardoff rapped.

Stinger Salvatore grinned evilly as he saw that flag.

"They couldn't take it," he chuckled. A wizened-faced lieutenant, beside him, shook his head.

"It's too easy, boss," he cautioned. "Watch out for a trick."

"Right!" agreed Stinger, and his unblinking eyes narrowed to deadly slits. "They plan to double-cross me again, probably. This time I'm going to do the double-crossing."

Hoskins's voice blared from a loudspeaker.

"There is no need for this killing, Stinger!" Hoskins bellowed. "There will be more millions than any of us will know what to do with. Together we can accomplish much. Will you talk business?"

Stinger's grin grew larger. "Sure, Hoskins, but not inside the factory. I've got to be careful."

"I will put myself at your mercy. I'll come out to talk with you," Hoskins declared.

The barrel-shaped figure of Hoskins appeared in the factory door. He walked out into the square. He was an excellent target in the strong searchlights.

From behind the queer shields, half a dozen Tommy guns were aimed directly at his body.

"Now," Stinger whispered to his lieutenant, "you go talk to him."

"Me?" Fear showed on the wizened one's face.

"You." Stinger's voice was harsh. A heavy automatic was in his hand. "And when you get near him, this is what you do." He talked rapidly.

"I'm sending my chief lieutenant," Stinger's voice rolled out. "He can talk for me."

An expression of disappointment flickered for a moment over Hoskins's fat face, and was gone.

The wizened criminal slipped from behind a shield and stepped forward. He licked his lips, darted furtive eyes to each side of him. It was apparent he did not like his assignment.

Ten feet from the barrel-shaped man, the killer whipped out a gun. Without warning he leveled it, squeezed the trigger.

Hoskins dropped. He waved one hand toward the window of the factory.

The ground shook as from a tremendous clap of

thunder. Lightning seemed to play about the big yard. Sparks of terrific voltage leaped from one antenna post to another. The entire yard became a field of electricity, of voltage greater than a thunder cloud.

The wizened thug died like an insect before a blowtorch. Those behind shields who had reached the outer limits of the yard withered and died, and turned into black, scorched things that had once been men.

A curse ripped from Stinger's tight lips.

Hoskins leaped up, ran unscathed from the scene of terror to reach the comparative safety of the factory.

"A double double-cross!" Stinger swore. "The blasted field has no honor!"

Stinger could not understand Hoskins's escape, either from the bullet or the terrible lightning that rained in the yard. Hoskins hadn't entirely escaped the bullet. But the little killer who had shot at him had been nervous; the lead had merely nicked the big man.

Had Stinger witnessed the scene in the cavern far beneath the earth, before Hoskins came to the surface, he might have understood why the barrel-shaped one could run through lightning unscathed. Then again, he might not have understood.

But one thing the flashily dressed gangster did know, and that was that the blasts of electricity which were barring his advance, were flashing from the antenna-like posts.

Grenades rained about those posts. The posts went down. The deadly lightning ceased.

Clement Hoskins's face was as nearly gray as it could be under the cherry-red complexion he now had.

Yardoff's sharp lips were tightly closed. His scarecrow figure was tense.

"A tight spot," he conceded.

Hoskins nodded. "Those damn grenades. And he was too smart to come near me himself in the yard."

The defenders were quailing, ashen-faced. Frantically Hoskins and Yardoff drove them to the windows, forced them to keep up a rain of machine-gun bullets.

Both Yardoff and his barrel-shaped companion had removed a glove. Sight of the waving, cherry-red hands alone kept the thugs at their posts.

A second blast furnace erupted, spraying molten glass, as an explosive bomb hit it.

"Let them have the factory," Yardoff ordered suddenly. "We can get them easier if they do."

Hoskins rasped a brisk command.

Thugs wasted no time. They raced frantically toward the elevator that ran beneath. There weren't so many left now. One load could take them all.

As Stinger's men rushed in above, the glass cage of the elevator rocketed downward. It stopped at the furnace level.

Yardoff leaped out, pressed a button.

There was a dull boom from above. Sand and rock rained down. The upper part of the tunnel collapsed.

"Let them dig through that," Yardoff sneered. "If they do, they'll find some nice surprises for them."

Hoskins nodded, soberly. "Right, but we've got to work fast at that. We've got to find Doc Savage at once, put the pressure on him."

Professor Torgle also was planning to put pressure on Doc Savage.

He had been amusing himself. Time after time he had swung his knife, to halt its razor-sharp point a hair's distance from the back of the bronze man's neck.

He wearied finally of the sport.

"No," he cackled—and prepared for a thrust that would drive the glass knife into the bronze man's heart.

It was then that Doc Savage moved slightly.

Professor Torgle's knife hand froze. The bronze man's body had not moved much, but it was enough.

"Alive," breathed Torgle. "Alive. The key to safety and freedom. And I—I thinking him dead, was about to destroy that key!"

Torgle scampered down the sheer face of the wall of fire as if pursued by demons. A twisting, grotesque grin was on his face; his flat head bobbed up and down.

He was drooling as he reached the Pit of Horror. He kicked one of the bodies contemptuously, and climbed up the ledge until he could reach the corridor that led to the big caverns.

Torgle reached the first group of workers. He whispered to them excitedly.

Incredulous looks were his answer. He argued.

"But—but the Pit of Horror!" gasped one. "We—we dare not go there. That is death!"

Professor Torgle spat. "Fools!" he cackled contemptuously, "you carry your death with you in your own body. The wall of living fire in the Pit of Horror cannot hurt you, because you are already living fire. The pit of death has merely been used as a bogy to frighten such fools as you. Those who have gone there have been shot down, not mysteriously killed. But you will die, die horribly, like a sheet of fire, unless you take the chance I'm offering you."

His words carried conviction.

The cherry-red men dropped their tools; they began to pick up pieces of glass that could be used for weapons.

Others carried the message through the cavern. A mob formed swiftly.

"We will get this Doc Savage, we will hold him for a hostage!" Torgle shouted. "We will demand that we be given the secret which will bring us freedom or we will kill the bronze man. If Hoskins and Yardoff don't agree, we will kill them, also!"

The mob started racing for the Pit of Horror.

"But why is the bronze man helpless there?" one convict asked, not unreasonably.

"I do not know, fool!" Torgle shouted. "We will learn. And I need help to bring him out."

"I can't stand it! I can't stand it!" a voice screamed suddenly. The shriek was high and despairing.

"Kill! Kill!" another shouted.

An insane spirit gripped the mob. In a moment they were changed to a mob of maddened, kill-crazy convicts.

They raced on ahead of Torgle. The queer-shaped professor tried vainly to halt them. He saw his plans evaporating under the kill-crazy frenzy of the mob.

Then something happened to him, too. He also was affected by the steady, never-ending hum. He screamed, scampered forward with the rest. He forced his way to the front.

Professor Torgle had become just another murder-determined man, racing at the head of the pack.

"Kill! Kill!" the men screamed. "Kill Hoskins! Kill Yardoff! Kill Doc Savage!"

Chapter XVI

A MOB AMUCK

Doc Savage heard the mob approaching. The bronze man stirred; his flake gold eyes opened.

He had been slammed so hard against the wall that the blow had knocked him unconscious. His head had taken a terrific shock, his entire body had been subjected to terrific punishment.

But his powers of recuperation were far beyond those of an ordinary man. Almost in the same instant his eyes opened, his brain cleared, became alert.

Instantly Doc acted. His hands went to his waist. About that waist was the emergency kit he always carried with him. In it were compact instruments of all kinds.

Some of those instruments were of metal. And it was the metal that had caused his predicament.

The wall of living flame had acted as a gigantic, tremendously powerful, electromagnet.

Electromagnets such as are used in handling of huge quantities of scrap iron are so powerful that they will lift a man from the ground merely by attraction to the nails in the bottom of his shoes.

The wall of living flame was even more powerful. It had literally jerked Doc through space in pulling toward it the metal that was in his emergency kit. As long as the bronze man had that belt around him, he was held suspended in the air.

There had been nothing of metal about Professor Torgle. He had escaped the action of the electromagnet.

Doc's fingers worked swiftly. They explored several pockets of the emergency kit.

The weird will-o'-the-wisp ball of fire, which had been dancing overhead, dropped lower, passed over the bronze man. He paid no heed.

The mob streamed over the ledge, dropped down in the Pit of Horror. Professor Torgle was in the lead. He had his glass knife.

Several of the more agile of the killers started up the wall. Doc loosened the strap on the emergency kit. His body floated down—dropped to land squarely in the center of the pack of murder-mad convicts!

There were more than fifty armed killers in the pit. More were dropping down every moment. It appeared sure death for one man to oppose that mob. No one person—not even Doc Savage—could hope to overcome all of them.

Doc Savage had no intention of trying.

His arms smashed out. Those nearest him were thrown back. They crashed into others, kill-crazy.

That was all the bronze man intended. It was enough.

In an instant the pit was a snarling, whirling mass of fighting men. Men fighting each other.

Doc had correctly interpreted the temper of the mob. Knew that they had to fight, would fight any one, even each other.

Glass knives rose and fell; blood spurted. The screams of dead and dying made the Pit of Horror live up to its name.

Torgle's crafty, maddened brain alone saw what was happening.

"It's Doc Savage!" he screamed. "Don't let him get away! Kill him! Kill him!"

Doc twisted through the screaming, fighting throng. Occasionally his fist shot out and some killer dropped, unconscious. It was impossible for Torgle to keep him in sight.

Suddenly one of the convicts on the edge of the crowd screamed. He pointed at the pile of skulls at the bottom of the wall of living fire.

The pile of skulls began moving. No one was near.

Then one of the skulls seemed to mount, unaided, into

the air. The vacant eye sockets appeared to be grinning in the ghastly, weird blue light.

The skull began to speak.

"Those who have died here resent your presence," came the words. The jaw bone clicked. "Leave while you yet have time."

Fear of the supernatural swept over the crowd. Mob spirit is infectious. It sweeps with amazing speed. The men scrambled, tried to climb up the ledge to get out of the cavern.

But just as quickly, they stopped, turned around.

Perhaps if they had not been maddened, the trick would have worked. Killers fear what they cannot understand. But this mob of murderers was past that fear. They returned to their one idea: Kill! Regardless of the cost, kill!

The mob swept toward the skull hanging in mid-air. That one they would even kill again. Professor Torgle's flat head was in the lead. His slit of a mouth was working strangely.

Then Doc Savage stepped into view.

The bronze man was dangling the skull from a black, invisible silken cord. A second thread was attached to the bony jaw. The supernatural was explained.

A yell of hate rose from the mob.

Doc Savage dropped the skull. He ran directly toward the mob.

Death seemed certain. Two score knives were ready. Some were thrown, to whistle dangerously close as the bronze man dived directly toward his foes.

Then one cabled arm shot out. The knife in Professor Torgle's hand clattered to the floor. Those near him were swept back by powerful blows.

The next moment Doc had picked up the queer-shaped scientist and had tucked him under an arm like some light bundle. As Professor Torgle kicked and twisted vainly, Doc whirled, raced away. The baying pack was in hot pursuit.

A wall of flame was in front. The bronze man dived through it. There was a thin, narrow trail. The trail skirted the edge of a mighty underground precipice.

The pit stretched down from there many hundred feet. Even the narrow trail did not go far. It ended in a thin line that not even a mountain goat could follow.

But Doc did not get that far. He took three quick steps. Then he seemed to lose his balance. Torgle cried out in horror.

Doc's feet faltered. Then he fell, taking Torgle with him, straight into the yawning pit below the precipice!

A howl of frustrated rage came from the pursuers. The more venturesome crowded to the lip of the cliff-like rock. They peered down, muttered.

Nothing was to be seen. The bottom of the precipice was so far below that it was hidden in the veil of blue.

"Doc Savage is dead!" howled one.

The cry was taken up by others. From disappointment they turned to glee. They danced, raved, swung arms aloft.

"Now for the others!" screamed a convict who had once been Public Enemy No. 1. "Let's get them, get them all, Hoskins and Yardoff!"

The tide turned. The convicts rushed backward, scrambling over each other in their haste to leave the pit.

"Doc Savage is dead. Doc Savage is dead! Kill Hoskins! Kill Yardoff!" they shrieked.

Up the long corridor they rushed, toward the great cavern and the lead doors they knew opened to the outer world.

Chapter XVII

BETWEEN TWO FIRES

Long Tom stared straight ahead. He could not even move his eyeballs. His lips had been caught half opened. He spoke through those lips, his voice strangled. One by one, he called out the names of the other four men in the room.

Johnny could only grunt. Ham's reply was smothered. Monk gave a faint squeal. Only one voice seemed freer than the others: That was Renny's.

"We are being held in an electrical field," said Long Tom. He articulated with difficulty. "You, Renny, seem nearer the outer edge than any of the rest. Try hard to move."

As Long Tom spoke, maddened shouts drifted through the closed door of the laboratory. The electrical wizard did not know what was happening.

But the tenor of the shouting of the convicts was not encouraging. The men were obviously out to escape— and to kill whatever lay in their path.

Renny's huge frame strained. Every ounce of muscle in his six feet four of solid strength strained in mighty surges to break the invisible bonds that held him.

"I can move a little, not much, though," he gasped. Perspiration was streaming down his severe, puritanical face.

Renny's huge fists clenched. He gave an exclamation of delight at the sign. It showed he was breathing through the invisible electrical field.

"Touch the wall, Renny!" Long Tom urged desperately.

The huge engineer worked like a man trying to swim in some heavy, clinging substance. Inch by inch, he worked one arm out. His outstretching fingers touched the glittering, luminescent wall.

There was a crackling noise. Sparks flew from the ends of Renny's fingers and the wall where he had touched it. The bonds that held him seemed to slacken.

Instantly, the big engineer threw himself hard against the rock where the luminescence was brightest. His already cherry-red face became more and more livid.

"Feel anything, Renny?" Long Tom asked.

Renny's lips moved spasmodically. He swallowed hard. The words seemed to choke from his throat.

"Feels like some one tickling me all over," he muttered. "Sort of a queer tingling."

"Good!" Long Tom snapped. Then he was silent for

a moment. Outside, the shouting was louder. The convicts were almost at the door of the laboratory.

Long Tom was sure the convicts would be as little affected by the electrical field as Torgle had been. He was sure they could come in and slash the five men with glass knives while they were helpless.

Sweat trickled down his face. His jaw was contorted, his own muscles strained to the utmost in a futile effort to escape.

"The button—the button Torgle pushed!" he gasped.

Renny lunged forward. He fought as though swimming against a strong tide.

"Kill them! Kill them!" came the roar of the mob. The roar came from just outside the laboratory door.

The big engineer gave a final, desperate lunge. He reached the button, pressed it.

The roar of the mob swept by outside. The convicts were surging down the corridor, on toward the main workshop cavern. Evidently they had not known Doc's aids were in the laboratory, or if they had known, they had forgotten.

Monk and Ham stretched strained muscles. Johnny slumped as the electrical field was shut off and they were freed from their living-statue poses.

Long Tom leaped up. "We've got to get to work, and work fast!" he bellowed. "Something has gone wrong, or Doc would have been here."

"Right," said Ham.

"What do you know about it?" Monk protested in mock anger. "You can't do anything but talk. But perhaps you'd better practice up on a good speech, for if that gang comes back here after us, it may take some good talking to save our lives."

"If that Torgle comes back here, I'm going to wring his blasted neck!" Renny said solemnly.

"And me—" started Johnny.

The door of the laboratory opened slowly. A misshapen figure with a twisted head showed in the doorway.

The twisted figure started to speak. His words were

drowned in a roar of animal rage from Monk. The homely chemist, his hairy arms outstretched menacingly, darted forward.

Renny was step to step with him. They reached the figure simultaneously.

Then a peculiar thing happened.

Monk was lifted into the air as lightly as if he had been a feather duster. Renny's big fist shot out, but whizzed through empty space. The two men charged again, slammed into each other with a force that almost knocked them both out.

"We should not fight against ourselves," Doc's voice said dryly. "That would impede our progress."

The amazement in Monk's eyes at the treatment he had received changed to wild delight.

"Howlin' calamities, Doc!" he squealed. "We didn't suspect it was you!"

Long Tom's shoulders lifted and fell. A smile of relief crossed features ordinarily pallid and unhealthy-appearing, now a bright cherry-red.

"I'm glad you're here, Doc," he said simply. "I think I know what this thing is all about, but what to do about it has got me licked."

"Doc's a spirit again," Ham jeered at Monk. "See, this time he returns to us as the spirit of Torgle."

"Shut up, you big-talking shyster!" the hairy chemist squealed. He danced about excitedly.

The tension was gone. Doc's aids didn't ask questions. It was enough for them that the bronze man was finally with them.

"What are our chances, Doc?" Renny asked.

The bronze man did not answer for a moment. He was busy assembling various pieces of equipment. He moved rapidly and without hesitation.

Long Tom watched him with the delight of a star pupil watching a master at work.

"What chance did you say we had, Doc?" Renny repeated.

"Many things are happening," the bronze man said slowly. "As to our chances—that I will know in a very few minutes. I am going to try an experiment. If it works, we have a chance. If it doesn't—"

There was silence for a moment in the laboratory. Doc's aids glanced at each other briefly. It was seldom they had heard the bronze man admit that they might not be able to get out of any jam in which they found themselves.

But they did not know all that Doc did.

The bronze man did not explain how he had escaped from the Pit of Horror. None of his men knew of his peril there, and he did not think it worthy of mention.

The escape really had been quite simple. Doc had seen a ledge beneath the precipice. The ledge was hidden so that only sharp eyes could see it at all.

When Doc had seized Torgle, he had leaped to that ledge and hidden. The convicts, peering down, did not know the ledge existed and missed it entirely. Doc had brought Torgle back to safety after the convicts had fled, donned his disguise and came to the laboratory.

The bronze man was working with startling swiftness. His aids stood silent, watching intently. From what Doc had said, and his actions now, they realized that their situation was indeed perilous.

The bronze man found zinc and copper plates carefully wrapped in pliant folds of malleable glass. He was careful not to touch the metal plates. He held them in glass tongs, suspended them in vats of acid.

Then he hooked them up in an intricate series of wiring. He pulled Long Tom's experiment apart, used much of the apparatus that was in it. He found half a dozen storage batteries with glass cases and from one corner pulled a huge electric motor. Its case was of glass. All metal parts were carefully covered.

The bronze man's muscles strained as he brought it into the center of the room. It was then that his men noticed his strange complexion.

They were cherry-red, but they appeared pallid compared with Doc. The bronze hue of his skin had been replaced with a fiery red glow more startling than that of any of the breechclothed men.

Doc hooked up the large motor. Then he walked silently to the other end of the complex circuit running through the zinc and copper plates in the acid vats. He paused for a moment before two large contact points of copper. He stood on a rubber mat.

Then it was that Doc Savage did a strange thing. He was pressed for time, he had been working with the utmost swiftness. But now he paused. Carefully he removed every bit of make-up, stood forth as Doc Savage, recognizable by all.

"If this experiment is not a success, do not try to leave the caverns," he said, and there was unexpected feeling in his voice. "You must barricade the door of this laboratory. Long Tom will continue to experiment until success has been achieved."

Long Tom leaped forward. Horror was on his face. He understood why Doc had removed his make-up, why he had spoken as he did.

Doc Savage was going to try a dangerous experiment. If he failed, he wanted Long Tom to know he was to carry on, wanted to look as his friend had always known him.

If the experiment did not succeed, Doc Savage would be dead!

Long Tom's tongue seemed to stick to the roof of his mouth. He dampened parched lips as he tried to speak. His voice came as if from a distance.

"Stop, Doc!" he cried. "Let me try it. You could carry on—"

Doc pushed him aside. Looks of understanding crossed over the faces of the bonze man's other aids. Monk would have stepped forward, would have tried to dissuade Doc by force, even though he knew it was useless.

Renny held him back. Sorrow was on the big engineer's thin, severe features. "He—he would do it anyway, Monk," he objected. "It's hard, hard for all of us, but there is nothing we could do."

Long Tom's figure was tense. He, more than any of the others, realized the chance Doc Savage was going to take.

The death of Z-2, the death of the escaped scientist in Doc's office, the fear the cherry-red men had shown for an ordinary stream of water, all pointed to one thing:

Each of them was carrying a lethal jolt of electricity in his body!

Long Tom did not pretend to know how to explain it. He only knew it was so. The human body always has a certain amount of electricity in it, and the cherry-red men in the cavern seemed charged so that they were almost walking dynamos. If they touched metal that was grounded, if they touched water so that it grounded their body, it brought their death.

They were doomed to die if they escaped. Only in this cavern, for some reason, were they safe.

And Doc Savage and all his aids were now cherry-red. It would seem logical that they would also face death unless they found something to counteract that peril.

The bronze man was going to try and experiment to see if he had solved the secret. If he failed, he would die. He would die as Z-2 had died, as others had died. He would die horribly, his body burned and scorched, his powerful muscles, his keen brain wiped out as a fuse is wiped out.

Doc's lips were set firmly. He reached out, seized the two contact points.

The smell of ozone filled the air. Acid in the vats began to boil.

The bronze man's muscles contorted in a mighty effort. An ammeter needle on a dial began to jump crazily. Wires glowed red-hot with the sudden burdening of terrific current.

Then the big electric motor began to turn!

It moved slowly at first, then began to whine with a sudden, mighty surge of power.

"Another extraordinary manifestation of electric phenomenon," Johnny muttered amazed, and gazed at Doc's face in sudden awe.

The ruddy hue of the bronze man began to pale, the natural bronze color of his skin appeared.

Doc's flake gold eyes were flashing. He watched another ammeter needle slowly drop toward the zero marks.

"Success!" Long Tom breathed, and it appeared to be the first time he had taken a breath since Doc had seized hold of the contact points. "Now if we only have time—"

Sudden shots sounded from the corridor outside. A Tommy gun roared in the distance.

It did not appear there was going to be time.

Things were happening in the big workshop cavern. It was an uproar, a surging mass of fighting, savage men.

Hoskins's fat face was worried, his sunken eyes frantic. Yardoff was fighting with grim, bitter enjoyment, his scarecrow figure relaxed, as if, now that a showdown had arrived, he really enjoyed a battle.

And a showdown was near.

The blast in the upper tunnel had failed in its work. It had not completely blocked the shaft. Stinger Salvatore's men had found an opening, had worked their way down.

And Yardoff and Hoskins, with the few loyal thugs they had left, were between two fires.

Salvatore's men, armed and deadly, were attacking from one direction. The maddened convicts, with glass knives for weapons, were attacking from the other.

"A tough spot," Hoskins panted.

"The convicts complicate things," Yardoff agreed. A smile that was scarcely human split his thin face. "If they were with us, if they would attack Stinger's men, it would soon be over. As it is—"

He lifted the Tommy gun he held in rubber-clad hands, brutally mowed down a group of cherry-red men who had started to rush forward.

Br-r-r-r-r-r-r!

Lead hammered the corridor wall. One of Stinger's gunmen had turned a bend in the corridor, almost had the range.

"We've got you, Yardoff! You and Hoskins better give up. Maybe if you do we'll let you live, even if I do take the millions you expected to get."

Stinger Salvatore's voice was triumphant and jeering. It seemed to the flashily clad gangster that he held all the cards.

One of Yardoff's eyebrows lifted mockingly. He moved to a lever beside the wall, pulled it.

The passageway behind became a solid sheet of flame. The gunner who had fired a moment before became a burned chunk of flesh.

Stinger bellowed in frustrated rage. The roar of a grenade sounded.

Yardoff shrugged. "It will only take them a few moments to blast down the electrical connections," he conceded. "We had better retreat."

Hoskins nodded. Sweat was running from him in long streams under the hot rubber suit he wore.

Cautiously they backed up. More of the cherry-red men appeared.

The thugs with Hoskins and Yardoff appeared as frightened of the cherry-red men as they had been of Stinger's killers. Their guns popped ceaselessly.

But the convicts were canny. The first burst from Yardoff's Tommy gun had brought some measure of sanity back to them. They lurked in passageways leading off the main corridor.

As the thugs passed, a cherry-red hand would dart out. That hand would touch one of the thugs.

The thug would yell once. Then he became very dead. Half-insane shrieks of glee from the kill-crazy convicts would follow.

"Kill! Kill! Kill!" they chanted.

"The end?" Hoskins asked. His lips trembled.

Yardoff surveyed him scornfully. "Of course not!" he rapped. "Stinger and his men will destroy themselves. They do not understand what they are up against here."

"Then what are we to do?" Hoskins was almost sobbing.

Yardoff lifted his Tommy gun, blasted a path through an approaching horde of cherry-red men. Behind them another grenade exploded. Exultant yells followed.

"We will simply get Doc Savage and his men, take

them to the submarine, and return when the fighting is over," Yardoff said.

His Tommy gun blared its song of death.

Chapter XVIII

A FLIGHT FOR LIFE

The roar of the Tommy gun was warning enough to Doc and his men that things had gone wrong outside. And it told them enemies were approaching.

"If I only had my sword cane!" Ham moaned.

"Or if we had some super-firers!" Renny shouted.

"I'll take 'em! I'll take 'em all!" Monk howled. He jumped up and down, beat his chest in perfect imitation of a bull ape.

"Shut up, you guys!" Long Tom put in swiftly. "Help Doc. He can't save us all if you don't work."

"We'll stand guard," Renny said, motioning at Ham. "We're no good on the type of stuff you're doing, anyway."

The bronze man said nothing. The situation was one of the toughest of many tough spots he and his men had ever been in, but work, not idling, was the only thing that would save them.

Monk, with Long Tom, grabbed more plates, more glass boxes, worked rapidly to put together additional batteries of the type Doc had made.

Johnny was pulling out additional electric motors, working swiftly to splice connections to them, careful to use rubber and glass only when he came in contact with the wires.

Doc was mixing chemicals in several glass retorts. He poured the resulting liquid into glass balls, plugged the openings.

Swiftly he handed half a dozen each to Renny and Ham.

A wide smile overspread the dapper lawyer's face.

He opened the door, tossed one of the glass balls down the corridor.

It landed not a score of feet in front of Yardoff and Hoskins.

There was a most satisfying explosion.

The barrel-shaped man and the scarecrow one almost went on their noses, so quickly did they stop.

Yardoff snarled, loosed a blast from his Tommy gun that played on the door.

Renny waited until the drum of the gun clicked empty. Then he jumped out, looped two of the glass balls down the corridor as if he had been a baseball pitcher.

Hoskins had raised a glass pistol. He shot, but he was so anxious to get away from there that he almost tripped over his own feet.

The two crooks raced back, until they could stand in the comparative safety of a small niche in the wall while they reloaded the Tommy gun.

Two more apparatus such as Doc had erected were ready for use now.

Monk seized the handles of one. Long Tom grabbed onto the other. Slowly the cherry-red color died from their faces; the queer, tingling sensation their skin had experienced faded. They felt more keen, more mentally alert than they had for some time.

"Hurry, Doc, hurry!" The cry came from Renny. The big engineer had left his post at the laboratory door, was rushing toward the back.

A cherry-red face had appeared around a bend. A hideous face, with lips drawn back over dirty teeth, with glass dagger held in one hand, only the glass dagger did not show its real color. It was dripping crimson.

"Give me those glass bombs!" Monk squealed. "You've got to get deloused!"

He reached out, almost touched Renny's hand. Doc shouted. Monk froze.

"Lay the bombs down, Renny, then let Monk pick them up," the bronze man said. "Had he touched you, he would have been killed."

Yardoff's submachine gun roared.

"Kill! Kill!" came cries from the cherry-red men.

Doc and his aids were surrounded.

Long Tom replaced Ham at the laboratory door. The dapper lawyer, Renny and Johnny, grabbed hold of the contacts to the queer, battery-appearing machines.

Motors hummed.

Monk suddenly squealed, came running back. "Out of bombs," he bellowed, "and one of those mugs almost touched me!"

Doc nodded. "It is time to go," he said.

And it was time to go.

Yardoff and Hoskins had discovered that although the glass bombs made a terrific roar, they were practically harmless. The cherry-red men were so inflamed they did not think of danger at all.

Doc ran toward the maddened convicts. His men followed.

A small, runty killer was in the lead of the pack. He was bleeding from a score of wounds, but his bloodstained hands bore mute witness that he had slain his share of victims.

The bronze man halted directly before him. The runty killer raised his knife.

Long Tom's breath came in sharply. Doc no longer was cherry-red; the electricity that had been in his body was gone. If the killer even touched him, that touch would be fatal!

One of Doc's hands shot out. It was sheathed in a rubber glove. It caught the killer's wrist, threw him back.

"Wait!" the bronze man said.

The average man could not have done it. It is doubtful that even Ham, with all his power of oratory, with all his knowledge of how to grip attention, could have done it.

But Doc Savage did. The horde stopped.

The bronze man's flake gold eyes swept over them. There was something hypnotic in his eyes.

"Look at me," he said. "Look at me carefully. A few

moments ago, I was cherry-red, even as you are. I, too, was doomed to death. I am not now."

A gasp of awe went up from the killers. The bronze man had seized the only thing, had said the only thing that would have halted their rush for long, that would have brought the light of sanity back to their eyes.

"My friends and I have solved the secret of how to get rid of the living fire," Doc said.

Behind him, Yardoff and Hoskins had reached the door of the laboratory. They paused for a moment, fearing a trick. But it could only be seconds before they smashed through. The bronze man paid no attention, spoke as if he had hours for the task.

"You will find three machines in the laboratory," he went on. "Three at a time, grab hold of the control handles that are attached to them. You will become normal, will no longer be walking dead men."

A scream of excited jubilation came from one of the killers. That was all that was necessary.

The next instant they were sweeping past Doc and his men, the thought of killing them forgotten.

Knives flashed again as they fought to be the first at the machines that would mean life if they could ever escape.

When Yardoff and Hoskins thrust open the laboratory door, Doc and his men had vanished.

Johnny tried to take the lead. He thought he knew the path that led to the submarine.

"If we get away now," Long Tom argued, "we can come back later, save what men are still alive. If we delay, we'll be dead and no one will survive."

Doc Savage nodded his agreement.

"You figured it out, Doc, you know what it is all about?" Monk asked pridefully.

"Of course he did, stupid, or we wouldn't have any chance at all!" Ham gibed.

Doc and his aids raced into a maze of tunnelways. Some of them were so low they could hardly pass through them. Others were high, and winding. Sounds of shooting and shouting became dim. There was only the steady, monotonous roar.

"I'm completely nonplussed," Johnny confessed.

"If you mean lost, I am, too," Long Tom said.

Doc moved in the lead. He turned in a direction that seemed directly opposite the right one to Johnny, but the geologist gulped and said nothing.

The six slid forward on silent feet. The noise of shooting grew more loud. Now and then a shriek could be heard plainly. Tommy guns roared. Occasionally there was the blast of a grenade.

Tension grew. For the first time in their careers, Doc and his men were completely without weapons. Cherry-red men might jump from any of the side passageways they passed. If they did, Doc and his aids would be helpless.

A face appeared ahead of them. It was the face of one of Stinger Salvatore's thugs.

The killer yelled gleefully; he yanked up his gun to fire.

Doc's hand shot out. A rock sped through the air with unerring accuracy. It caught the killer on the nose. Blood spurted, blinded him.

Howling vengefully, the thug opened fire. But he could not see. His shots went wild.

"Come," said Doc.

If the six had moved fast before, now they fairly flew. Doc did not seem to hesitate. Without a second's pause he moved from one corridor to the others.

The bronze man had not been to the submarine, but that appeared to make no difference. And it didn't. From the slant of the passageways and the geological structure of the walls, Doc figured out the only direction in which the underground stream would lie.

And if his men had felt tense before, now they felt doubly so. Not only were Petrod Yardoff and Hoskins after them, not only would they most likely die if they encountered the cherry-red convicts, but they knew Stinger Salvatore would realize that he could not let them escape alive, that he would go to any length to stop them.

A sigh of relief was wrenched suddenly from Long Tom. A heavy door had loomed ahead.

Monk squealed happily. Before Doc could stop him,

he raced in the lead, grabbed at the lock on the door.

There was a sudden flash. Monk was hurled through the air, to land sprawling.

Ham raced to the hairy chemist's side. "Monk! Monk!" he pleaded. "Speak to me! Speak to me!"

"Why should I, you overripe specimen of a razor-back pig?" Monk's words came weakly—but he could speak.

Ham leaped to his feet. He was as nearly flustered as it was possible for an astute lawyer to be. It always embarrassed him when Monk caught him showing emotion of any kind.

"You—you. I'll slit your gullet when I get my sword cane back!" he raged.

"The machines did not take all the electricity from our bodies," Doc explained. "I was afraid that they would not, since we did not have time to do a thorough job."

The bronze man took a small glass bottle from his breechcloth. It was one Long Tom had watched him fill while he was in the laboratory.

Quickly, Doc poured out liquid. He ran it from the tip of one finger, up his arm, across his shoulders and down the other arm.

Without hesitation he stepped toward the door. He placed one hand on the ground. With the other he touched the metal.

There was a streak of flame. It followed exactly the path of the liquid. Doc was unhurt. He opened the door without difficulty.

"Juice will seek the easiest conductor," Long Tom explained to Renny. "What juice there was left in Doc shot out along the line of liquid metal, without hurting him."

The second door was also opened easily. In front of them lay the submarine, deck awash in the huge, subterranean stream.

Sounds of fighting came clearer behind them. Their pursuers, battling among themselves, but each eager to grab Doc and his men, were growing closer.

"Safe!" Johnny shouted. He raced along the tiny wharf to the sub.

Doc delayed a moment, a faint frown creasing his bronze forehead.

There was no sign of life about the submarine.

Johnny threw up the hatch, dropped down inside. The others followed.

As Doc landed, men seemed to pour out onto them from all sides.

They were the sailors who handled the sub. Some held deadly guns. Others were armed with heavy wrenches.

Chapter XIX

THE SUB AFIRE

Somewhere near by a girl screamed. It was the voice of Virginia Hoskins.

"Help! Help!" she cried.

A gun was pointing directly at Monk. The gun went off when the hairy chemist jumped at the man behind it.

Ordinarily Monk respected a gun. He knew how quickly one could end the life of even the strongest man. But the pure terror in Virginia Hoskins's voice had made him forget all ordinary caution.

His long, apelike arms swinging, animal noises coming unconsciously from him, the hairy chemist went into battle. He knocked the sailor out with one punch, turned hungrily for more.

Ham was jabbing with the scientific accuracy of the trained boxer. He missed his sword cane, but he could fight just as well as the average-trained ring man.

Renny's huge arms were working piston-like. His bony monstrosities of fists crunched jaws or skulls with equal facility.

Renny was probably the poorest fighter of all Doc's aids, but he was far better than average. And he was giving an excellent account of himself.

The engineer was frankly angry, not so much at the attack, as at what that attack might mean.

Renny wanted to come back to the underground caverns when he could work uninterrupted, when he could have time to study the queer gelogical strata, prepare papers on it that would confound his scientific associates.

He did not approve of being trapped at the last moment, of losing out when all seemed won. He was expressing that disapproval with straight rights and lefts, interspersed with a few well-aimed kicks at shins.

Doc alone seemed to be taking no very active part in the melee. And that was strange. For ordinarily the bronze man was in the front rank, leading even causes that appeared hopeless.

The bronze man's eyes swept the room of struggling figures. The room was small, the fighters were constantly getting into each other's way. Knuckles aimed for one jaw quite often smacked the jaw of another.

And creeping toward them, hard faces set in sardonic lines, were two men carrying submachine guns!

The fighters were between Doc and the approaching killers. He could not get at them. Soon those weapons would swing into action.

And from the look on the faces of the men carrying the guns, they wouldn't care if a few of their own men got killed, as long as Doc and his crew were wiped out.

"Cease fighting! Drop to the floor!" Doc roared.

Monk groaned; Renny seemed to want to argue. But none hesitated.

Doc's aids did not know what it was all about, but they trusted the bronze man implicitly. Without hesitation they dropped.

Br-r-r-r-r-r-r!

A Tommy gun spoke. Slugs tore over the heads of Doc's aids. It was aimed directly at the bronze man.

He was no longer there. He had dived through a hatchway behind him.

Some sailors tore frantically in pursuit. Others paused to tie up the five men who had dropped to the floor.

Renny's face was a study. He did not need to be told

why Doc had acted as he had, but he liked a fight almost as much as Monk did, despite his disapproving features.

Doc had seen the killers approach, his men realized, had known some of them might be killed, even if they could overcome all their foes in the end.

And the bronze man would try any strategy rather than permit one of his aids to be killed.

His strategy was now plain. He had drawn all attention to himself, was willing to play a lone hand against the dozen or more men who were on the boat.

A man with a short, black beard—the one who had first conducted Long Tom and Johnny before Yardoff— issued crisp instructions, his beard bobbing energetically.

"The bronze devil cannot get off this boat," he said in his queerly accented voice. "He is the one Yardoff most wished. Try to get him alive if possible, but if not—kill him. He is dangerous."

Ham was forced to grin. "Blackbeard" evidently hadn't heard all the fighting in the big caverns, did not know that possibly by this time Yardoff had no interest except in his own safety.

But it was understandable that the sailors did not know. The doors leading into the caverns were thick and heavy. Noise could not be heard through them.

The searchers went to work swiftly but cautiously. They knew their boat, knew every possible hiding place, and hiding places are not so many on pigboats where every inch of space must have its use.

One by one, those searchers disappeared. At first their absence was not noted.

They would drift toward the battery room, enter— then all sign of them would cease. Each of them was armed. It seemed unlikely that even if the bronze man were hiding there that he could overcome them all without at least one being able to fire a warning shot.

The black-bearded leader returned to the control room. His eyes were puzzled as he noticed how few men he had left. He called. There was no answer.

The puzzled look was replaced by one of slight alarm. He sniffed the air.

"Gas!" he rapped suddenly. "The bronze devil has gotten to the chemicals in the battery room, has made a gas!"

The black-bearded man raced toward the battery room. His remaining sailors were at his back.

"Be careful," he warned, "Savage is tricky. He may have figured out a way to save himself."

He thrust open the door, stood at one side, gun ready. His mouth dropped open.

Inside the battery room, the floor was covered with sprawled figures. In the center of those figures was the big form of Doc Savage.

"S-strange," the black-bearded man muttered.

A peculiar expression crossed his face. He turned, tried to flee. His legs would not carry him. He slumped, went down. Behind him, sailors crumpled to the floor.

Above, Doc's five aids were bound and tied so that they could not move. The gas from the battery room spread toward them.

Nor were things going well for those in the caverns.

The big, bluish-lighted rooms held mute evidence of the carnage that raged. Of the more than one hundred convicts who had been alive less than an hour before, fewer than two score remained.

Stinger was practically without aid. That puzzled him.

Weapons that his men had carried had suddenly turned into death agencies for their owners. Flame had spurted, the killers had died.

Stinger did not know that the bodies of his men had become filled with electricity, that the metal of the guns had caused death-dealing shocks. But he had been smart enough to throw his gun away when he saw electrical sparks play along the weapons of others.

He found a glass pistol, went on. The humming noise of the caverns, the wild screams of the maddened convicts, acted on the flashily dressed gangster's nerves, also, but he did not know it.

He thought he was sane, that every one else was crazy.

A group of cherry-red men plunged into view. In

front of them, running for his life, was the barrel-shaped figure of Clement Hoskins.

Stinger Salvatore's lips were back, his unblinking, steely eyes filled with desperate purpose. He pulled the trigger. Hoskins staggered. The bullet had caught him high up, near a shoulder.

A smaller man would have gone down. Hoskins did not. He proved that his big body was not fat, but the powerful, solid muscle he had bragged about.

A deadly grin wreathed his moon face. He brought his own gun up carefully. As Stinger fired a second time, Hoskins pulled the trigger.

Lead from Stinger's gun plucked Hoskins's sleeve. Hoskins scarcely noticed it. A third eye appeared in Stinger's forehead. This eye was unblinking, also. But it was not steely, it was black that rapidly changed to crimson. He was dead.

Yardoff was running down the corridor that led to the submarine. He was pursued by several of the cherry-red men. Their flashing knives foretold his fate if he was caught.

Clement Hoskins lumbered after them. He ran slowly. He could not run fast. His strength was seeping from the bullet wound in his shoulder.

A queer, misshapen figure slid into the corridor almost at his back. The man had an almost flat head, with little, deep-sunken red eyes.

"Hoskins!" called Professor Torgle.

Hoskins turned with a snarl. It was then Torgle leaped, plunged his knife deep into the barrel-shaped man's heart.

Clement Hoskins was dead, but he did not know it. One of his hands reached out, caught Torgle by the wrist, held him fast. The other encircled the misshapen man's throat. Slowly that fist tightened. Torgle scratched and kicked, he clawed and fought.

Hoskins went down. Torgle went with him; strange, strangling noises came from his throat.

After a while they both lay still.

Petrod Yardoff was more clever. He tricked his pursuers by dodging off, taking a winding passageway.

But he made one mistake, too. He did not take time to close the doors when he passed them.

Panting, he came through the second door, saw the submarine resting peacefully on the subterranean stream.

He paused, looked behind him for a moment, took off a rubber glove to wipe his forehead.

It was at that moment that Doc's big figure rose from the group of sprawled men in the battery room. An oxygen tablet in his mouth had saved the bronze man from being overcome, while the others had dropped.

Swiftly he turned on blower fans. The gas he had concocted with chemicals in the battery room brought quick unconsciousness, but its effects would not linger long.

Then the bronze man raced to the control room, freed his men.

"Tie up the sailors," Doc said calmly. "Then get to your posts. We are ready to leave."

As his aids rushed to obey, Doc looked out the conning hatch.

It was then Petrod Yardoff saw him.

The scarecrow man realized Doc and his crew had seized the submarine, that all his own plans to escape had been blocked. He knew then that he was lost.

But he knew something else, too, knew one final trick that would carry those who had blocked him to death.

An almost insane shriek came from his lips. He leaped to a switch beside the lead door. He shoved the switch home.

Instantly, water began to boil about the submarine. A wire carrying a tremendous load of electricity had been hooked to the pigboat. In a moment its plates became red-hot.

It was a flaming submarine of death!

Chapter XX

JOURNEY'S END

Doc had only an instant of warning. He saw the switch as Petrod Yardoff lunged toward it.

"Stand on rubber!" the bronze man shouted. His voice penetrated every part of the submarine. His men heard. They obeyed.

Several of the unconscious sailors were touching metal. It was unfortunate, but there was no hope for them. They were electrocuted instantly, dying as if they had gone to the electric chair for murders they had committed.

The submarine was rapidly becoming unbearably hot due to the tremendous current that was running through the metal, and the strong resistance of that metal.

Something had to be done, and done fast, or motors inside the pigboat would become worthless.

A terrible leer was on Petrod Yardoff's face.

Doc went into action. A diving suit was in one corner of the control room. Evidently one of the crew had been inspecting the bottom of the mysterious stream.

With dazzling speed, the bronze man donned the suit. He grabbed a pair of wire-cutting pliers. The handles were taped, but that seemed slight protection against the enormous flow of electricity that must be coming into the submarine.

The wire was fastened near the nose of the sub.

Doc took a long breath, popped out of the conning hatch. The next moment and he was running down the top of the sub, had slipped into the water.

The water surrounding the pigboat was so hot the diving suit immediately became a turkish bath. Steam clouded the glass.

Working blind, the bronze man fumbled for the wire.

Frantic cries were coming from inside the submarine. It was becoming unbearably hot there. And Doc's aids did not know what was happening, did not know whether the bronze man had escaped or not.

The pliers encountered the wire. Sparks flew.

With steady hand, Doc slipped the cutters over the wire, applied pressure.

Despite the tape on the handle of the pliers, despite the rubber gloves of the diving suit, a sudden surge of electricity went through the bronze man's body.

He was thrown in the air, tossed about by the mighty, invisible force.

Doc's lips came together hard, his flake gold eyes almost closed. With the last ounce of his strength, he pressed the pliers home.

The wire parted.

It was seconds before the bronze man recovered enough to scramble back on the boat. Yardoff stood as a man amazed. His last hole-card had failed.

Once more he wiped perspiration from his forehead. He took a step toward the boat—and halted.

Monk and Renny appeared out of the conning tower. Renny's face was grim and merciless. Monk gave a sigh of relief as he saw that Doc was uninjured.

It was then that the surviving cherry-red men appeared.

They came running through the lead door noiselessly, running as a wolf pack runs when the kill is near. A terrible sound came from their throats as they saw Yardoff.

The scarecrow man screamed—once.

As far as he could see there was death behind him and death in front of him, for he could not understand that others might be more merciful than he, that Doc might save him.

"Back to your posts, prepare to dive," Doc Savage ordered his aids.

There was an unusual note of urgency in his voice. Monk looked wonderingly. He could not see what could cause the bronze man to speak so when all seemed won.

Then he saw what Doc had seen seconds earlier, and for once he lost his color. He was almost trembling as he raced into the submarine. And Renny was right behind him.

"Come on, Yardoff! Come now!" Doc shouted.

Petrod Yardoff hesitated. He looked behind him. The pack of cherry-red men were almost upon him. Their weapons were raised.

Certainly there was no mercy there. There might be some hope with Doc. Yardoff made up his mind. He raced forward, out on the tiny dock toward the submarine.

Had he looked behind him, he would have seen a strange thing then. The cherry-red convicts had halted. They tried frantically to yell. Their voices seemed paralyzed.

With one accord, they turned, raced back in the direction from which they had come.

But Yardoff did not see. He stretched out one hand, grabbed a rail to lift him up.

There was a sudden sheet of fire. Flame played over the scarecrow body of the man who was playing for millions.

The odor of burned flesh came into the air. Petrod Yardoff died as others had died from the living flame. He died from a trap of his own devising, only he had made it for others.

He had forgotten to replace his rubber glove after he had wiped his face.

Doc glanced once more at the shore. The long, electricity-charged wire he had cut was still dancing. Sparks were flying from it. Those sparks had already done their work well—too well.

A fuse was flaming slowly. It was leading under the leaden door where buried explosive lay waiting.

"Crash dive!" ordered Doc.

The submarine shuddered. It smashed downward, under the water, as its tanks were thrown wide open to fill at once.

"Full speed ahead!"

Doc gave the order before the submarine could reach the bottom of the subterranean stream. He knew he must do so.

And barely in time.

There was a muffled roar, a noise that did not echo loud inside the submarine, now under water and nosing toward the outlet that led to the sea.

But if the noise was not loud, the results of that noise more than made up for any lack of sound.

There was a rush of water. The submarine was lifted up, hurled backward as if by a gigantic hand. Its propellers raced; its motors labored.

The explosive under the leaden door evidently had been buried deeply enough so that water from the stream was released into the underground cavern.

Possibly the blast opened up a new passageway into the lower depths of the land of living fire.

Only the fact that the submarine was in the big stream saved it. Had it been caught in a narrow passageway, even its strong hull would have been crushed under the beating it would have taken.

As it was it was almost an hour before the surge of waters passed, before the battle for safety finally ended.

Then Doc headed toward the open sea.

Virginia Hoskins was still pale. She had passed through much. But her cheeks became a faint pink when she saw the admiring gaze Monk could not keep from his face. The girl had escaped being electrocuted by standing on a rubber mat after hearing Doc's warning.

Doc turned over the controls to Renny, let the big engineer show his stuff as he piloted the way through the twisting tunnel, fought against the surge of the tide.

The bronze man with the others relaxed in the ward room, relaxed for the first time in hours.

"Now will you tell me what it was all about?" Monk demanded.

Doc nodded. "As nearly as possible," he said. "To begin with, I think Yardoff and Hoskins first discovered the wealth of native mineral in the upper passageways of the cavern. A majority of those minerals, particularly pyrites, are vital to the munitions industry.

"Many nations are arming. Some wish to hide that fact. If they bought in the open market, they could not keep it secret. Yardoff was once an agent for an international munitions firm. His reputation was shady. Hoskins contacted him. Together they smuggled out the minerals they had found."

"Bootlegged it by submarine," Ham said with satisfaction.

"Then they discovered the lower cavern, the cavern with the living fire. The ore there, as we all know, was highly charged with electricity. It operated the furnaces of the glass factory; the very ore itself provided light.

"But they needed men to work there, men who would not talk. Hence the prison breaks which they engineered with the Stinger's help. That is where Z-2 came in. As an F.B.I. man, he was investigating a Federal prison break. He tried to get away, and knew something of the peril he faced, but even then he died."

"But," objected Long Tom, "where did Hoskins and Yardoff hope to profit? They could have used the ore for power, that would have brought them a fortune, and legitimately."

"Yes," Doc agreed. "They could. But did you not notice how hard and how heavy that ore was? If they could have learned how to smelt it, how to work it, so that it would have been used, they would have had an impenetrable armor plate, something worth many millions."

"So that's why they wanted us!" Johnny gasped.

The bronze man nodded. "Without doubt, that is why."

Virginia Hoskins shuddered. "But I still don't see where the horrible living-fire death came in."

"The ore has strange electrical qualities," Doc explained gently. "The longer the human body was exposed to it, the more electricity it absorbed, until the convicts were walking dynamos. If they touched anything that grounded them, they died. If they touched a person not affected as they were, that person died. That was apparent from the first. Z-2 touched an oil barrel with his bare hand. The man at the office had the sole of one shoe eaten away by quick-acting acid. Hoskins and Yardoff, however, evidently had a battery arrangement much as we used to de-electrize themselves."

Johnny wet his lips. "A-and what was the ore, Doc?" he mumbled at last.

"You are a geologist, Johnny. Don't you know?"

"I think I do. I am almost afraid to say."

"But you are right, you must be right," Doc said. "We were privileged to be among the first to see the ore that comprises the core of the earth. There was a bulge there, one that brought that core comparatively close to the surface.

"No one else has ever seen it, although scientific tests prove it must be of the hardness and density that we found. It could have changed the history of the world—made into armor plate. The nation that owned it would be unbeatable."

"I-I'm going to take a vacation!" Monk blurted suddenly. His eyes were on the beautiful face of Virginia Hoskins. "When we get out, I'm going to visit Palm Springs, that is—" He gulped, became as vivid a red as he had appeared in the cavern.

"He means," Ham explained maliciously, "that he is going to visit there if you are anywhere near, Miss Hoskins."

"I am going there, also," Johnny said. "The phenomenon must be investigated. I wish to probe further the strange working of the labyrinth."

But Johnny and Monk were mistaken. Johnny lost all interest in Sandrit and the desert when he read the first newspaper he saw as they returned to civilization.

The newspaper told of a strange eruption that had occurred on the desert.

Citizens of Sandrit were quoted as telling of a strange gun fight that had preceded the eruption, but authorities were inclined to doubt that.

But a glass factory owned by Clement Hoskins, who was missing, had suddenly been swallowed by the earth. In its place was a huge, bubbling stream, heated by some strange, subterranean force. And queerly, the water was salty.

The sea had hidden nature's secret.